THE SECRET OF THE LOST TUNNEL

DIFFICULT assignments are nothing new to the Hardy boys and this one that takes them to the Deep South is particularly challenging. Their mission: to vindicate a long-dead Confederate general, disgraced during the Civil War because he was accused of stealing hidden gold belonging to a bank.

In a museum exhibiting relics of the Civil War, the brother sleuths find a puzzling clue that may help to clear the general's name and pinpoint the location of the hidden gold. But a dangerous criminal and his cohorts are out to steal the treasure and constantly harass Frank and Joe and their pal Chet Morton.

Skillfully avoiding booby traps and flying bullets, the boys persevere in their perilous quest. The arduous search is full of surprises that will thrill all fans of the Hardy boys.

"Get out!" the man roared

Hardy Boys Mystery Stories

THE SECRET
OF THE
LOST TUNNEL

BY

FRANKLIN W. DIXON

NEW YORK
GROSSET & DUNLAP
Publishers

CONTENTS

THE SECRET
OF THE
LOST TUNNEL

CHAPTER I

Double Warning

THE telephone in the Hardy home rang sharply as the clock struck four. Blond-haired Joe bounded into the hall and took the call.

"Fenton Hardy's residence," he said, and in answer to a query, "My father isn't home. Will you leave a message?"

"This is Dr. Bush," the man informed him in a deep voice. "You're going to have a visitor. Watch your step and pay no attention to his story. He's dangerous. He's out of his mind." The man spoke a few seconds longer, then hung up abruptly.

Puzzled, Joe returned to the living room.

"What's the matter?" asked his dark-haired brother Frank, who was a year older.

"A General Smith is coming here. Dr. Bush, who just phoned, says the general's crazy, and that we should pay no attention to him."

Before Joe had a chance to explain further, the telephone rang again. He answered it.

"Hello?" Placing his hand over the mouthpiece, he whispered to Frank, "A woman—says she knows Dr. Bush." Then into the instrument he said, "Yes. . . . Yes. . . . Why? . . . Hello, hello!"

The click on the other end of the line was evidence the woman had ended the conversation.

"Who was she?" Frank inquired.

"Didn't give her name," Joe replied. "But listen to this. She said if we heard from a Dr. Bush we should call the police immediately."

"Good night!" Frank exclaimed. "A mystery to solve before we even see the people involved in it!"

But puzzling situations were nothing new to the brothers. As sons of Bayport's famous detective, Fenton Hardy, they had encountered many baffling cases, beginning with *The Tower Treasure*. In their most recent adventure, *The Sign of the Crooked Arrow*, Frank and Joe had successfully concluded an intriguing mystery.

Now the boys' thoughts were interrupted by the sound of the front doorbell. Joe opened the door. Before him stood a man in the uniform of the United States Army. On his shoulder he wore the single star of a brigadier general.

"I'm General Smith," he said. "I'd like to see Mr. Hardy."

"Step in, please," Joe said politely. He shot a quick glance at Frank, then surveyed the stranger carefully.

The general, whether mentally unbalanced or not, had all the bearing of a fine military man. He was of medium build and stocky, with a ruddy complexion, blue eyes, and red hair.

"My father's not here," Frank told him.

"That's too bad. How is he?"

"Why—er—very well," Frank replied.

"Wonderful man," General Smith commented.

"You know him?" Joe asked.

"Surely. I came to speak to your father on a very important matter."

"We could give him your message," Frank offered. "I'm Frank, and this is my brother Joe. Dad's been away. We expect him back some time today."

General Smith walked into the living room and seated himself in Fenton Hardy's favorite club chair, looking keenly at the boys.

"I'll relate my story briefly," the man said. "You can tell your father, in case he doesn't get back before I return to Washington. It concerns a treasure buried during the Civil War. I want him to find it."

Joe stole a glance at Frank. His brother looked puzzled as the man continued.

"My great-grandfather, a Confederate general," he said, "was disgraced during the Civil War because he lost a bandoleer containing a special cap box made of silver."

"Bandoleer?" Joe asked.

"Yes. A military shoulder strap. Today they contain cartridges. The old one my great-grandfather lost carried a small silver box which was a family heirloom."

"What was so disgraceful about losing that?" Frank asked as he observed the man intently.

"The box contained no bullets," the general explained. "But it did hold a secret which has remained unsolved to this day. You see, just before a certain battle, my great-grandfather called at the plantation of his cousin, Beauregard Smith, a wealthy planter and president of the local bank. Beauregard confided to my great-grandfather that if enemy troops got too close, he intended to bury his gold, together with that belonging to the bank."

"What happened then?" Joe put in eagerly.

The man moved uneasily in his chair. "Just before the Battle of Rocky Run," he went on, "an old slave from Beauregard Smith's plantation ran into Great-grandfather's headquarters. He handed him a sealed envelope moments before dropping dead from exhaustion."

As the visitor stopped speaking, he sprang from his chair and paced rapidly toward the door.

"What's he going to do now?" Frank wondered, recalling the telephone warning.

But the general turned sharply on his heel and walked back, continuing his story.

"Great-grandfather had time only to glance at

"My case concerns a Civil War treasure!" said General Smith

the message. It contained a series of numbers. Sounds crazy, I know."

Joe gulped and looked at his feet.

"Across the face of the message," the general proceeded, "were the letters C S A. But before Great-grandfather could study the numbers, scouts brought reports of the enemy's approach, and Great-grandfather had to issue a call to arms. He hurriedly hid the message in the ammunition box. The opposing sides joined in battle shortly afterward, and the fight continued into the night. In the darkness and confusion, the bandoleer and the cap box disappeared, and with them the secret."

"Didn't Beauregard Smith remember the message he had sent?" Frank asked.

The general stared absently at the boy, then went on, "He was killed defending his plantation. The place was cannonaded and burned to the ground."

The general started to pace again.

"Beauregard Smith's family was penniless, and in disgrace, too, because the bank's gold was lost. They accused my great-grandfather of taking it for his own use!"

Joe gave a whistle. "Some accusation!"

At that moment the telephone rang again, startling the general and the boys. Frank leaped to answer. The caller was Dr. Bush.

"Has Smith arrived?" he asked abruptly.

"Hold on a moment," Frank said.

In the silence that followed, Frank strained to hear any familiar sound that might identify the place from which the doctor was calling. In a second he was rewarded. The words "Two on a raft!" boomed in the distance. The voice of Pete down at Shorty's Diner!

Frank beckoned to Joe and whispered, "Bush is at Shorty's Diner. I'll try to keep him talking while you get a look at him."

Joe raced from the house and hopped into the brothers' convertible. He drove speedily toward Shorty's Diner, located a few blocks away in the downtown section of Bayport. Reaching it, he hastily parked, bounded up the front steps, and pushed open the door.

As the tempting aroma of sizzling hamburgers and coffee drifted to Joe's nostrils, he glanced quickly toward the telephone booth at the end of the long counter. It was empty!

Slowly a rotund youth sitting on a stool swung around. In his hand he held half of a triple-decker sandwich.

"Hello, Joe," he said. "What's the big hurry?"

"Chet!" Joe exclaimed. "Did you see anybody come out of the phone booth a second ago?"

"Don't rush me," Chet pleaded, and bit into the sandwich.

Chet Morton, a pal of the Hardys, enjoyed eating, and did not like to be hurried while engaged in his favorite pastime. Joe was bursting with impatience as he watched Chet chew contentedly on the big mouthful.

"This is awful important," Joe pleaded. "Not another bite, now." He repeated the question.

Chet gulped, patted his lips with the white paper napkin, and said, "Sure I saw the guy. Came out of that booth so fast he bumped into me. I said 'Look, mister, you almost knocked the sandwich out of my—!' "

"For Pete's sake, Chet, cut out the gab! Where did he go?"

The stout boy wheeled around on the stool and pointed to the side door. "Thataway. What's up, Joe?"

"Tell you later." Joe raced through the door, then halted on the sidewalk. Chet lumbered after him.

"I think that's him down the street there," Chet volunteered. "He was tall and wore a dark suit. Carried a black bag."

Without a word, Joe sped after the figure who was now a block away. The stranger glanced back, then broke into a trot. At that moment a black sedan slowed up at the corner. The man hopped in. Before Joe could catch up with him or get a look at the license plate, the car disappeared.

Joe turned dejectedly as Chet arrived on the scene. "Didn't even get a good look at him," Joe moaned.

"Is he a crook?" Chet asked, puffing.

"Maybe. Anyway, somebody asked us to get the police after him. I wish I hadn't lost him."

"Don't worry, pal," Chet piped up. "I figured this was another detective case, so I decided to help you."

"How?" Joe blurted, a frown creasing his forehead.

"Surprise," Chet replied. Then, for the first time, Joe noticed that his plump friend held an old camera in his hands.

"I took his picture," Chet said proudly.

CHAPTER II

The General's Enemies

CHET Morton grinned as he handed the battered camera to Joe. On the front mount was a telescopic lens.

"I got a telephoto snapshot," Chet boasted.

"Are you sure?" Joe eyed the camera skeptically. "Where'd you get this?"

"At a pawnshop," Chet explained. "Just because it's secondhand doesn't mean it's junky."

Joe examined the camera. The lens seemed good enough, but the camera body had been cracked, and was patched here and there.

"I hope it hasn't any light leaks," Joe said, handing the camera back to Chet. "I'd sure like to have a picture of that man!"

"Count on me," Chet said as the two boys drove toward the Hardy home to develop the picture. "You fellows working on a mystery?"

Chet's voice contained a note of apprehension.

The Hardy boys were his closest friends, and although Chet greatly enjoyed their companionship, he was always loath to participate in the risks they ran.

"I don't know yet," Joe replied, and explained hurriedly about the mysterious telephone calls.

At the house Frank met them at the door. "Did you find Dr. Bush?" he whispered excitedly.

Joe shook his head, then Frank explained in low tones that the man had ended their telephone conversation very abruptly.

After hastily introducing Chet to General Smith, Joe ushered his friend into the basement, where the Hardy boys had their darkroom.

"You'll find developer and hypo under the bench, Chet. I hope the picture's good."

While Chet was busy removing the film from the old camera, Joe rejoined his brother and General Smith.

"I must say," the general commented, "that you boys sure dash around."

Frank apologized for the interruption and explained, "Our friend Chet's a photographer and uses our equipment sometimes. Please go on with your story about the Civil War, General Smith."

"Well, when my great-grandfather as well as my grandfather failed to clear up the mystery, my father took a hand, because the Beauregard Smith branch of the family still blame us for the loss of their fortune."

Frank and Joe sat tensely on the edge of their chairs, listening.

"My father was a general, too," their caller said. "The military tradition in the Smith family has been our pride for over a century. That's why I'm determined to find the treasure!"

General Smith thumped the table beside him so hard the lamp on it teetered precariously. He jumped from his chair and again began to pace the room. The boys looked at each other in alarm. Seating himself, the general continued:

"After exhaustive work, my father was able to unearth the fact that the bandoleer had been stolen by a spy. Long after the war, when there was no longer need for secrecy, the story came out that an enemy soldier, named Charles Bingham, had entered my great-grandfather's camp. He was seen during the battle, but later was reported missing."

"And the secret of the buried gold with him?" Joe inquired excitedly.

"That's right," the general answered.

"You want Dad to help you find the hidden gold," Frank assumed. "The only clue is Bingham, and you don't know what happened to him."

General Smith nodded. "I know it'll be hard, but I have a lot of faith in your father's reputation."

"Dad's the best detective in this part of the country," Joe said. "You came to the right man. But Dad will want proof of your story before—"

The look which flashed across the general's face was ample evidence Joe had said the wrong thing.

"Proof!" the man sputtered. His red hair fairly bristled.

"General Smith," Frank said, "my brother meant no offense. After all, we haven't seen your credentials."

"Credentials!" the general shouted.

Suddenly the crackling atmosphere was interrupted by the click of a key, and the front door swung open. In strode Fenton Hardy.

"Dad!" Frank exclaimed, hurrying toward the tall, broad-shouldered detective.

"Boy! Are we glad to see you!" Joe cried out.

As Fenton Hardy entered the living room, General Smith made a sudden move toward him. "Fent Hardy!" he boomed.

To Frank and Joe's amazement, their father stood stock-still a moment, then put out his hand, exclaiming:

"Jack Smith!"

Frank and Joe stared wide-eyed as their father and General Smith exchanged greetings.

As soon as he could, Joe took his father aside and whispered, "Dad, we were told the general is insane!" The boy quickly related what had happened.

The detective, recovering from the shock of the announcement, pondered for a second. Then he laughed heartily and put his arm around his son.

"Tell General Smith what you just told me, Joe."

Upon hearing the insanity story, General Smith threw back his head and laughed heartily.

"It only goes to show you can't tell who's crazy. I've thought ever since I came here, Fenton, that your sons were acting rather peculiarly!"

Grinning like a couple of boys, Mr. Hardy and General Smith recalled the happy days they had spent together one summer in an officers' training camp.

Frank turned to the general finally. "General Smith, have you any idea who Dr. Bush and the woman caller might be?"

"Not the faintest," General Smith answered, a worried frown creasing his forehead.

"My guess is," Mr. Hardy spoke up, "that Bush is no doctor and he's using a fake name." He turned to the general. "Did you tell anybody you were going to visit me?"

"Not a soul."

"Did you make a memorandum that someone might have seen?"

"No. The only thing I did was write the letter."

"Letter?"

"Yes. Don't tell me you didn't get it!"

The general said that he had made a quick trip down to Centerville, the town nearest the old Beauregard Smith plantation. While there, he had discovered that someone had been digging secretly on the property. At once he had decided to enlist

Fenton Hardy's help and had written him a letter.

"Then somebody intercepted the mail," Mr. Hardy surmised, "and learned you were coming here."

The detective asked General Smith for a resumé of the strange story of the missing bandoleer. While he was telling it, Frank and Joe went to the darkroom to see Chet. They found him gazing at a wet print.

"Hey, this is only half a picture!" Joe exclaimed, peering at it. "Nothing but the doctor's legs and a black bag."

Chet was crestfallen. His telephoto camera had failed him. "Guess I'll just tear this up and start all over again," he said glumly.

"Don't do that!" Frank interrupted. "This might prove to be a valuable clue."

Chet went back to work on the rest of the film, and Frank and Joe returned upstairs.

Mr. Hardy and the general were still discussing the mystery. Their Aunt Gertrude, Mr. Hardy's spinster sister, who lived with them, had come in, and heard the story.

"No good will come of this," the boys heard her prophesy as they entered the living room. "The minute I heard a warning was involved—"

"Now, Gertrude," Mr. Hardy spoke up, trying to calm her, "we've dealt with mysterious phone calls before."

"That woman means big trouble," said his sister, who was apt to jump to conclusions. "And as for that doctor— Oh, my pie's burning!" She rushed from the room.

"What I'm afraid of," General Smith said, " is that the secret message in the old bandoleer has been found and some criminal knows where to look for the gold."

Mr. Hardy set his friend's mind at rest on this score. "It's possible the message has been found, but if the gold cache had been located, Dr. Bush wouldn't be on your trail."

"If he's a crook, he probably has a criminal record," Frank suggested.

"That's logical thinking," his father said. "We'll go up to my study and take a look at the pictures in my rogues' gallery. Jack, you may recognize somebody you've seen in Centerville. Maybe it will give us a clue."

The four trooped to the second floor. The detective spread dozens of pictures over his desk. The general scanned each one carefully but concluded he had never seen any of the shady characters.

"I must get back to the hotel now," he said. "It's been—"

His words were lost as a shrill shriek sounded downstairs. Aunt Gertrude!

Frank and Joe leaped to their feet and bounded down the stairs. To their amazement, they saw their aunt grappling with two men at the front door. With her eyeglasses dangling wildly over one ear, Miss Hardy clutched one man by the hair and tugged at the other's necktie.

"You . . . can't . . . come . . . in . . . here, you ruffians!" she cried, blocking them. "Help! Help!"

"Hold 'em, Aunt Gertrude!" Joe shouted.

Then the men spied the reinforcements.

The thugs, whose faces were screened by the melee of arms, wrenched loose, and dashed into the street with the boys close behind.

CHAPTER III

Trouble on the Road

At the curb stood a black sedan, its motor racing and its door open. Before the Hardys could reach it, the fugitives jumped inside and the car roared away in the dusk.

"That's the car that picked up Dr. Bush!" Joe exclaimed. "And look, its license plate is covered with mud!"

The boys gave up the futile chase and returned to the house.

"One of those thugs might have been Dr. Bush," General Smith declared when he heard about the car.

But Joe was doubtful, and mentioned Chet's photograph. "The doctor has long legs and neither of those fellows did."

Mr. Hardy was trying to quiet his sister and at the same time get her story of the intruders.

"Those—those scoundrels said they were attendants from a mental institution," Aunt Gertrude spluttered. "Said General Smith had escaped and they wanted to take him back. I said he was a friend of ours, and they couldn't come in!"

"What did they look like?" Mr. Hardy queried.

Aunt Gertrude peered over her eyeglasses. "Do you expect me to fight off two cutthroats and remember their looks at the same time?" she asked crisply, her fright gone. "I was too busy to notice, but one seemed a young man about twenty-one. He had a nice, smooth complexion." Miss Hardy closed her eyes and shuddered. "Imagine such a young fellow trying to fight me! What is the world coming to!"

"We'll find them, Aunt Gertrude!" Joe vowed.

"No, you won't," their aunt protested. "You'll not go chasing such criminals. Oh, I knew when that woman telephoned, you should stay out of this! General Smith, we expect you to stay for dinner."

As Aunt Gertrude slumped into a chair, General Smith said he would be glad to stay and talk things over.

"You see how things are, Fent. Will you handle the case for me?"

"Yes," the detective replied evenly. "Finding the lost gold may be a thousand-to-one chance, but it would give me great pleasure to nab the two thugs who just tried to break into my house!"

"Fine!" the general boomed. "You'll start immediately?"

"Not so fast, Jack," Mr. Hardy said. "I must return to Washington tomorrow to testify in a case."

General Smith looked disappointed. "But suppose Bush finds the gold before we do?"

"We'll take care of that," Mr. Hardy assured him. He turned to his sons. "You fellows can start South at once to lay the groundwork."

"Frank and Joe?" asked the officer in amazement.

"Yes, indeed," Mr. Hardy replied proudly. "My boys help me on many cases. Sometimes they solve them before I do!"

"But this is different," continued the general, still hesitating. "This may be dangerous." He tugged at the lapels of his tunic as if he were trying to make up his mind about something. "Then I'll accompany them to Rocky Run! I have a short leave due. We can stay at my house on the outskirts of Centerville. How soon can you boys start?"

"Will tomorrow be soon enough?" Joe asked eagerly.

General Smith smiled. "I can see no burglar would catch you boys napping!"

"We can stop overnight on the way," Frank mused, "and make Rocky Run some time the next day."

A few minutes later Chet, who had been unaware of all the commotion, ran up from the basement, waving a photograph. "Hey, how do you like this one?" he asked enthusiastically.

"It's a picture of a car with the license plate covered," Frank remarked. "How'd you happen to snap it?"

Chet beamed. "It's the one Dr. Bush rode away in."

Joe reached for the picture as Chet, bursting with pride, said, "Guess I'd make a pretty good detective myself, eh?"

"This same car was outside our house a short while ago," Mr. Hardy told Chet, and related his sister's encounter with the two thugs.

Then Frank and Joe told their friend of the planned trip to the South. Chet's face fell.

"Gee, just when I thought we were going to have some fun with my camera, you're going away."

Frank, winking at his brother, said, "Say, Chet, you know we might need a good photographer on this case. How would you like to come along?"

"Oh boy!" Chet beamed. "I might even get to photograph the other half of that crook!"

The general smilingly agreed to take Chet with them, and the boy hurried home to pack.

"We'd better do some packing ourselves," Frank told his brother. They went upstairs.

Their mother, who had been out shopping and had just returned, looked in on them.

"Good gracious!" exclaimed the attractive

woman, amazed at the piles of clothes on the bed. "Another trip?"

The boys told of their plans. She smiled knowingly.

"I'll miss both of you. Are you taking the proper clothes?"

"We'll be outdoors most of the time," Frank replied, "exploring an old battlefield."

At the mention of a battlefield, Aunt Gertrude, who had come upstairs, burst out, "You're taking too much risk. Why, there may be hidden shells that might explode. And that heat down South—watch out for sunburn! Dinner's ready."

Aunt Gertrude, who had the habit of hopping from one subject to another, hustled downstairs to the kitchen. Her cooking was as savory as her language was peppery. As a special treat for Frank and Joe, she had baked an apple pie. When she brought in the dessert, the boys were delighted.

"Goodness knows when you'll eat properly again," she said tartly. "At least you should start this trip well-fed!"

General Smith thanked the Hardys and said good night shortly after dinner.

Later, the boys were deeply engrossed in their books of Civil War history when three loud knocks sounded on the front door.

"That's Chet," Frank assumed, recognizing the signal the boys used. "Guess he has some news that couldn't wait until tomorrow."

As Frank opened the door, four laughing young people burst into the Hardy home. In the lead was Iola Morton, Chet's sister, with Callie Shaw and Helen Osborne following. Chet brought up the rear with two large packages.

"Surprise!" Callie called gleefully. The pretty, blond girl, a special friend of Frank for several years, took a big white cakebox from Chet and set it gingerly on the hall table.

"This is a bon voyage party," announced black-haired Iola, Joe's favorite date, who was just as slender and good-looking as her brother was rotund. "Here. Take this bag, Joe. But be careful. It's soda pop."

Frank and Joe carried the refreshments into the kitchen while Helen and Chet went to find the boys' latest dance records.

"Don't y'all forget," Iola teased Joe, "to bring back a good Suthin accent."

"We'll leave that to your brother," Joe retorted, grinning. "He-all can learn it while he's eatin' fu-ried chicken."

After chatting about the trip and dancing until ten o'clock, the young people sat down at the dining-room table for refreshments. Then, bidding fond farewells to the Hardy boys, the girls left with Chet and chugged home in his old jalopy.

The following day, prior to their departure, the three boys sat down with the general and Mr. Hardy to discuss the mystery.

"This is like briefing troops before a battle." The officer smiled. He gave the boys a layout of the territory around Rocky Run. "It's not going to be easy finding the treasure," he added.

"I have a feeling you may run into trouble," Mr. Hardy remarked. "You boys must be constantly on the alert. Gold is always a source of—"

Suddenly a splintering crash cut the air. A dark object, hurled through the window, hit Frank full on the chest!

Quickly Joe dashed outside, but no one was in sight. Then he returned to the living room, where Mr. Hardy was holding a large heavy stone.

"That rock could have killed Frank if it had hit him on the head!" Aunt Gertrude declared hotly.

In a few minutes Frank was able to breathe more easily. A bruise on his chest was the only apparent injury caused by the mysterious assailant.

Why would anybody want to hurt Frank?" asked Mrs. Hardy, still trembling from the shock.

"I don't think Frank was the target," the detective replied. "I'm sure the stone was meant either for me or General Smith."

"To keep you from looking for the gold," Frank put in.

"I doubt whether it's worth while to call the police on this incident," Mr. Hardy said. "The fellow is probably far from here by now. But one thing is evident: your movements, Jack, are being carefully watched by some dangerous criminals. I'd advise you to lay low today and wait till tomorrow morning to start South."

It was agreed that both Chet and the general would stay overnight at the Hardy home to insure an early start the following day. By morning Frank was himself again, and eager to be off. While the group ate a hearty breakfast, Mr. Hardy had two of his operatives check the neighborhood for suspicious characters who might be spying on the Hardys. None were found.

Shortly before dawn, with farewells ringing in their ears, the Hardy boys, Chet Morton, and General Smith set off.

Chet looked very adventurous with his camera slung over a shoulder and a folding tripod in a leather sheath which hung from his belt. With Frank at the wheel, they rode out of Bayport and soon their sporty convertible was miles out on the state highway.

The boys found the general an interesting companion, with his stories of military life. Presently getting down to details of the lost gold, they discussed the message which was their only real clue. They all agreed on the possibility that the C S A stood for Confederate States of America.

"Before we do anything else," Frank said, "I believe we ought to look over the battlefield and the plantation."

Late that afternoon the four travelers reached

their stopover point. They registered at a large hotel, in the basement of which was a garage. When Frank drove the convertible inside, he said:

"I'm leaving it for the night. My brother or I will call for it in the morning."

The group registered, ate dinner, and went to bed early. After breakfast the next day Joe went for the car and presented the claim check.

"Listen, bud, nobody's takin' the car except the guy who left it," the attendant declared.

"I'm his brother."

"Yeah? So was that other boy his brother."

"What are you talking about?" Joe demanded.

"I'll discuss it with the guy who drove the car in here," the attendant insisted.

Seeing it was useless to argue, Joe went off for Frank. When they returned, the garageman related that a young man not much older than the Hardys had come in half an hour before, saying he was one of the Hardy boys.

"He didn't have a claim check," the man said, "so I wouldn't let him take the car."

"He was trying to steal it!" Joe exclaimed.

"What did he look like?" Frank asked.

"Blond. About your age. Wore blue pants and a sport shirt."

Frank thanked the garageman, and the brothers climbed into the convertible.

As Joe drove out to pick up Chet and General Smith, both Hardys had the same thought. Aunt

Gertrude had said one of the intruders at the house had been very young. Had the boys been trailed?

Out on the highway once more, the travelers amused themselves with the car radio as the miles rolled by. As usual, Chet became hungry long before the others. Seeing a pleasant-looking restaurant with a sign *Southern Fried Chicken*, he begged them to stop.

An hour later, having had a delicious lunch, they were on the road again with Frank at the wheel. After a few miles, as the beautifully verdant countryside slid past, Frank looked into the rear-view mirror.

"See that car back there?" he asked Joe, who was beside him.

His brother turned in the seat and peered behind. A black sedan was following a hundred yards back.

"It looks as if it's trailing us!" Joe said.

Frank slowed down. When the other car did likewise, he speeded up. The trailing sedan kept pace.

"I don't like this," General Smith said.

Scarcely were the words out of his mouth when the Hardys' engine began to sputter. As Frank guided the vehicle up a gentle hill, the accelerator suddenly failed to respond. He steered to the side of the road, losing speed all the while.

As he did, the sedan suddenly shot forward

alongside the Hardy car. In a split second it cut sharply in front of the car. Frank jerked the wheel quickly to the right and jammed on the brakes.

Joe was hurled against the windshield. Chet and the general pitched halfway over the front seat.

The car skidded on the sandy shoulder of the road, its front wheels teetering on the brink of a deep gully!

CHAPTER IV

Spies

"THROW your weight back!"

Frank shouted the warning as the car balanced on the edge of the gully, ready to topple over at any moment. When it had settled precariously on the sandy loam, Chet cried:

"We're lucky no one was seriously injured!"

"We're not safe yet," the general pointed out.

"Climb into the back, Joe," Frank directed. "Then I'll try to get out this door."

With catlike movements, Joe slowly crawled over the back of the seat to sit beside Chet, who was quaking with fear.

"Nice work," said General Smith, approving Frank's plan.

The added ballast in the rear made it safe for Frank to open his door.

"Hold everything for a second," he said. "I'll get a rope from the trunk compartment."

He pulled out a sturdy towline and tied one end to the rear bumper and the other to a nearby tree.

"Okay!" he called. "It's fast."

With a long whistle of relief, Joe opened the right-hand door and stepped out. Chet and General Smith followed.

"Whew!" said Chet. "Maybe I should have stayed home to take pictures!"

Moments later Frank flagged down a big van on the highway. When he explained the situation, the driver maneuvered his truck into position, Frank and Joe untied the tow rope from the tree and attached it to the rear end of the truck. Then the driver eased the boys' car to the edge of the highway.

"Guess you'll be okay now," he said. "There's a gas station about a mile up the road."

They thanked the man, who said he was glad to have been of service. As the truck rumbled off, Frank lifted the hood of the convertible and examined the motor. With Joe helping, he took the carburetor strainer off.

"Water in the gas line," he announced, noting the telltale cloudy substance.

"Somebody must have put in the water while we were parked at the restaurant!" Joe declared angrily. "And I'll bet it was one of Bush's men!"

Frank nodded. "He was probably in the car that was trailing us."

The general wiped his brow. "Well, boys, I hope we won't be meeting any more trouble—at least until we reach Centerville."

The Hardy car sputtered along to the service station. There the watery gasoline was quickly drained, the fuel line cleaned, and new gas put in. The foursome were ready to set off again in less than an hour.

Mile after mile raced beneath the wheels of the convertible as it steadily neared the old battlefield named for the stream Rocky Run. Late in the afternoon they drove through the little town of Centerville. The main street, paved with red brick, was flanked by two rows of huge live oak trees. Behind them, quaint old houses stood in the shade of spreading magnolias.

Farther on, the street led to a square, along which sprawled a handful of stores, a small stately courthouse, and a tall-pillared hotel. A solitary, bewhiskered man sat on the porch of the hostelry, smoking a pipe and rocking.

"Looks mighty sleepy around here," Chet remarked. "I think I'm going to fit right in with this life!"

"A peaceful old town," the general replied, smiling. "My place is a quarter mile down the road."

Frank drove on, and presently the general pointed out a driveway, which cut through a thick hedge of boxwood.

"Here's headquarters," the officer said as Frank stopped before a yellow clapboard house with tall, shuttered windows and doors, nestled far back from the road.

"What a swell place!" Chet exclaimed. "I'm going to sit under this big tree and eat and sleep—"

"I thought you were the official photographer on this mission," General Smith said, his eyes twinkling.

"Correct!" Frank agreed as they carried their luggage into the house. "Hup, two, three, four! Come on, Chet. There's work to be done."

The general's home consisted of a long living room, dining room, library, a kitchen, and three big bedrooms on the second floor. General Smith ushered the boys into the largest of the bedrooms.

"You Hardys will bunk here," he said. "Chet can have the next room."

"Pretty fancy bunks," Frank remarked, eying the two mahogany four-poster beds and the silk hangings at the windows.

"When do we shove off on the offensive?" Joe asked.

"Not until tomorrow morning," the officer replied. "I'd like you boys to get acquainted with Centerville first."

"What I want to know," Chet piped up, "is when chow is!"

"Follow me." The general led the way downstairs and into the kitchen. He opened the door of a shiny white refrigerator. The shelves were laden with food.

"Wow!" Chet exclaimed. "How did this happen?"

"Centerville's grocer has a key to my house," the general explained. "I sent Mr. Oakes a wire instructing him to provide for four hungry fellows."

The boys set to work preparing the evening meal. When they finished eating, General Smith suggested they set off for a tour of the town.

Evening was casting long shadows on the square when they arrived in Centerville. The general pointed out several large houses which dated from the Revolution, then stopped to talk with two men lounging on the hotel steps. When he returned to the boys in the car, he looked troubled.

"My friend Jeb over there says he's seen some strangers roaming around town," the officer began as they drove off. "Maybe Bush. I don't like it. Few tourists visit town this early in the summer."

When they returned to the house, General Smith and the boys discussed plans for the following day.

"It seems to me," Frank said, "that the best way to try locating the missing bandoleer would be to reconstruct the movements of the spy Bingham."

"Good idea," the general agreed. "Tomorrow we'll go to the farmhouse where my great-grandfather had his headquarters. The main part is still intact; it lies just off the battlefield."

"Is anybody living there?" Joe asked.

"No. It's now a county museum with an old Negro caretaker."

Joe, yawning, said he was going to try out the four-poster bed so he could be fresh in the morning. The rest followed him upstairs.

The next morning after breakfast the general, his two young detectives, and their "photographer" drove to Rocky Run. Low, undulating hills spread before them as they approached the battlefield.

"It wasn't as still and peaceful as this in 1863," General Smith remarked, surveying the fields and woodlands. "Well, there's Great-grandfather's headquarters."

Frank drove up to the old building and let the motor idle. What remained of the one-story farmhouse was in fair condition, with wisteria vines blotting out parts of the red brick. Off to the left stood two stone pillars, which apparently had supported a porch. On the right could be seen the crumbling remains of a side wing. Two windows stood bleakly on either side of a large door which bore a metal sign *Rocky Run Museum*.

"We'll park here," the general said. "Now, figuring that the spy Bingham left this spot with the bandoleer, which way would he go?"

While Frank and Joe pondered the question,

Chet said, "Mind if I get out and walk around?"

"Go ahead," Frank said. "Maybe you'd like a few pictures of the old place."

Chet's thoughts, however, were not entirely on photography. The movements of the spy Bingham intrigued him. This was one Hardy mystery which really had fired his imagination.

The boy circled the museum, then started to climb a little hill toward a clump of trees at the top.

"I bet Bingham went right up here to get a better view of the battle," he said to himself. He continued to walk around, looking out across the hills.

Suddenly Chet had the uncomfortable feeling that he was being spied upon. He stood still a minute, and heard a rustle in a thicket far off to one side.

Chet's heart thumped. It could be some kind of animal—or a person scouting their every movement. The stout boy considered the alternatives. He could race down the hill to report his suspicion to Frank and Joe. Or he could carry on by himself and turn the tables on the lurking enemy. Chet chose the latter. He'd try to snap the picture of the hidden foe!

He listened again, but all was still. As silently as possible, he unlimbered his camera, attached the telescopic lens, and cautiously approached the bushes.

At first the boy saw nothing. Then, through his telescopic view finder, he saw the blurred image of a man. Chet slowly retreated a few paces to avoid being seen as he adjusted the focus. The next moment he heard a stir in the brush and the figure fled.

At the same time, Chet, still retreating, stepped back into space and disappeared!

CHAPTER V

Retracing History

"HELP!" Chet shouted, flinging out both arms as he felt himself falling.

Frank, Joe, and the general, still mapping their strategy in front of the old headquarters, heard the cry from the knoll.

"Chet's in trouble!" Frank yelled, and started running.

The others kept close behind him and arrived on the scene almost at the same moment. There was not a sound.

"Chet! Chet! Where are you?" Frank called.

When there was no answer, the Hardys became alarmed. The general walked toward the edge of the woods. In a moment he called: "Here he is!"

The officer dropped to his knees beside a deep hole, the opening of which was nearly concealed by a growth of low bushes and grass.

"I've got one of his legs. Give me a hand with the other, boys."

Frank leaned far over and grasped the other leg. Together he and the general pulled Chet to a sprawling position on the level ground.

"Wh-what hit me?" Chet spluttered, still a bit dazed.

"Nothing hit you," General Smith replied. "You fell into a dry well."

As Chet rubbed his head ruefully, he told them he had tumbled while trying to get a picture of the fleeing figure.

"Where'd he go?" Joe asked excitedly.

"That way." Chet pointed to the right. "He— Hey! Where's my camera?"

Frantically Chet began combing the brush. The others joined him in the search. Minutes later, Chet shouted with relief.

"Here it is!" he cried, lifting the mechanism out of a patch of soft grass. "And not a scratch on it!"

"What about the man you saw?" Joe persisted. "Are you *sure* you saw one?"

"Sure I'm sure," Chet replied, ruffled by the implication.

"What did he look like?" Frank asked.

"I didn't get a good focus on him."

"And he's far away by this time," Joe said ruefully.

Frank and the general pulled Chet to level ground

As the group started back to the farmhouse, Frank noticed Chet was limping a little and asked if he wanted to go back to the general's house.

"I'll be okay," the boy answered. "I wonder where that spy Bingham went. What do you fellows think?"

Frank and Joe shrugged. "I'd like to hear the story of the battle first," Frank said. "General Smith, will you explain just where the troops were stationed?"

The officer turned to a hill beyond the one from which they had come, and with a sweep of his arm, said, "That ridge was held by the Northern troops. They had three lines of riflemen, backed by a strong force of artillery."

"They pushed down the hill and captured your great-grandfather's headquarters?" Joe surmised.

"Not exactly. It was in sort of a no man's land. The Southern troops were in this valley when the attack began. They retreated to that ridge over there." He pointed to another hill a mile away which was higher and steeper than the one the Federals had held.

"If Bingham got into your great-grandfather's headquarters," Joe continued, "all he'd have had to do would have been to hide until the battle was over."

"It wasn't as easy as that," the general said, smiling at Joe. "Great-grandfather had a force of cavalry in reserve. They counterattacked on the left flank and cut a wedge into the opposing forces."

"So Bingham was checked from going straight back to his own lines," Frank mused.

"It seems to me he wouldn't have had a chance to get through that line of cavalry," the officer agreed.

"Then Bingham would have had to go around the cavalry and along the Rocky Run," Frank reasoned, "until he could contact his own forces again."

"That's good thinking, Frank," the general said. "If he did go along the Rocky Run, he probably ran into more trouble, because artillery, which was rushed to my great-grandfather's aid, opened up from the opposite ridge. From all accounts, it was a terrific onslaught."

"He might not have come out of it alive," Joe commented. "But if he did, I think he'd have gone in the direction Frank indicated."

"True enough," the general stated.

"Then let's follow that trail!" Joe exclaimed.

"Remember one thing," General Smith said. "A good soldier makes the most of natural cover. Bingham would have made his way behind trees, boulders, along depressions in the ground, and behind slight rises to afford protection from the artillery. Well, let's start!"

"Gosh," Chet said, "I never thought of that. I think I'd go in a beeline just as fast as I could!"

"What a target you'd be!" Joe teased as they started on the trail which Bingham might have taken. Frank led the way, and the general nodded approvingly as the boy picked a route which provided the least exposure to cannon which years before had thundered from the ridge across the valley.

"You're a natural-born soldier, Frank," the officer said, smiling.

The trek was hot and arduous. Finally they came to the bank of Rocky Run.

"I think Bingham would have followed the stream here," Frank observed.

"Right," the general agreed. "He'd have tried to put the water between him and that daredevil cavalry."

"Hey!" Chet shouted suddenly. "There's a bridge Bingham could have hidden under!"

They came in sight of a span which carried the main highway over the Rocky Run.

"Only that's a concrete bridge," Joe countered. "It must have been built long after the Civil War."

By this time the four were within a stone's throw of the span. Suddenly a black sedan whizzed over it, the driver glancing down in surprise at the three boys and the officer. The car brakes jammed on, bringing it to a screeching halt out of sight of the searchers.

"That looked like the same sedan that tried to wreck our car!" Frank cried. "I'm going after it!"

He made his way up the side of a steep embankment to the edge of the bridge. Just as he spotted the back of the driver's head, the car's wheels spun and the automobile streaked down the highway with a roar. The license plate on the back of the car was still covered with mud, hiding the numbers.

"Where do you suppose he was going?" Joe asked as he and the others reached the top of the embankment.

"The road comes to a fork up there a way," General Smith said, pointing. "One branch runs past the Beauregard Smith plantation."

Frank whistled. "I'll bet Bush was in that car, and is on his way to the plantation!"

"Let's hurry there!" Joe exclaimed.

"It's quite a walk from here," the officer warned. "And a long hike back to our car."

"One of us can go for the car," Joe said.

"Let me," Chet offered.

Frank gave him the keys. "If we don't get to the plantation before you do, pick us up on the highway."

Frank, Joe, and the general set off down the road toward the plantation. When they came to the fork, they took the left one and were halfway to the Civil War farm of the Smith family when a horn blew behind them. The Hardy convertible rolled to a halt and the hikers got in.

"I thought you were lost," Joe remarked as they drove on. "What happened?"

"Nothing," Chet replied. "I just stopped at that little store along the highway. Here. Have some candy."

He thrust a bar into the hands of Frank and Joe, then turned to the officer.

"Will you have some, sir?" Chet asked self-consciously.

"Thank you. I'd like it."

Chet grinned. "I didn't know whether generals ate candy bars or not."

"I guess all men have a sweet tooth," the officer said, smiling. "Besides, soldiers eat chocolate before combat to get extra energy."

Chet looked askance at the general. "I prefer to eat my candy in peace and quiet."

Frank winked at Joe. "You may need some for battle right now, Chet. Never can tell what may happen if we run into Dr. Bush at the plantation."

At General Smith's directions, Chet presently eased the car off the highway and onto a rutted trail overgrown with weeds. There was no sign of the black sedan or any evidence that a car had recently entered the lane.

"This was a fine place once," the general said. "Those boxwoods over there are all that's left of a wonderful garden which stretched from the road to the mansion. My father had pictures of the old place."

At the general's suggestion, Chet stopped the car alongside a low, crumbling wall.

"Look over there," the man continued, extending his arm in a gesture toward a cluster of large oak trees which seemed to form a military phalanx. "That's where the big white house stood."

The ruins of the old mansion were scarcely visible through the tall grass and brush, which acted as the scar tissue of time to cover the wounds left by the war. The four got out of the car and pushed through the weeds toward the area.

The officer stopped and held his two hands parallel in front of him. "The steps to the front portico were right here. They led into the beautiful center hall of one of the most picturesque homes in the whole South.

"And look what's left now—nothing," General Smith remarked sadly. "Nothing but ghostly memories."

"And a cache full of gold somewhere around here," Frank reminded him, turning his thoughts to the work at hand. "General Smith, was the cellar of this place ever searched?"

The officer looked intently at the mass of overgrown rubble before them and mopped his brow with a handkerchief. "It's been searched at one time or another by three generations."

"And they found nothing?"

"Not a thing. That's why somebody has been digging elsewhere on the plantation trying to find the gold."

The four walked around in silence for several minutes.

"I think the first thing we should do is investigate the old farmhouse headquarters that's now the museum," Frank said at last. "We might find a battlefield relic that would provide a clue. Maybe Bingham even hid the bandoleer some place in the old building, and it hasn't been found yet!"

"Good logic," General Smith agreed after a pause. "I can see you're a better detective than I am."

Joe grinned. "You can't live with Dad all your life without learning something about sleuthing."

"Let's go to the museum immediately," Frank continued. Then, seeing a distressed look on Chet's face, he added, "I mean after lunch."

They made their way back to the car and drove to Centerville, past green fields of tobacco which bordered either side of the road.

"I think you boys can do your checking without me," the officer decided when lunch at his house was over. "I have a little business to attend to in town."

Chet, who was sleepy from having overeaten, would have liked to take a nap, but the boys urged him to accompany them. Half an hour later they drove up to the museum. Frank parked and they entered the front door of the erstwhile farmhouse headquarters.

"Just think," said Joe in awe, "once old General Smith and his staff walked through this door just as we're doing."

Inside the doorway the boys were met by an old Negro wearing a gray uniform similar to the Civil War uniform of the Confederate Army. He had a kindly, wrinkled face and a fringe of snow-white hair.

"Welcome to our little museum of the Battle of Rocky Run," he said pleasantly.

Frank noticed a sign stating that the museum was run by the County Historical Society and that a small admission was asked. He paid for the three of them.

"We'd like to look over the relics," Joe said eagerly.

"Help yourself," the old man said with a flourish of his hand as he sat down again. "This house is full of things they dug up from the battlefield."

The boys stood for a moment taking in their surroundings. Pictures of famous battle scenes and historic plantations covered three walls, while a huge fireplace with its carved mantel occupied most of the remaining wall.

Frank walked to one of the exhibits. "Look at these pistols," he said, bending over a table to examine a collection of many shapes and sizes.

"Here's something that'll interest you," Joe said to Chet. "Some Civil War photographs."

The boys turned their attention to the wall, where half a dozen rare old pictures showed a local encampment just before the Battle of Rocky Run.

"Don't forget we're looking for a clue to the old bandoleer," Frank remarked.

"You'll not find a clue here!"

The words boomed from behind the boys. They whirled around to face the speaker, who had appeared as if out of nowhere.

He was a tall, thin man whose long, sharp nose was accentuated by a broad black mustache and flowing black hair. Dressed in the costume of a plantation owner of the Civil War period, the man looked as if he had stepped out of one of the museum pictures.

"I'm Professor Randolph," he stated with a deep voice, "and why are you boys trespassing on my property?"

"We understood this was a museum, Professor, open to the public," Frank explained.

The man raised his eyebrows and with a half-smile said, "It was a museum until I bought it. You see, I'm a doctor of philosophy. I'm writing a book on the history of the Civil War so I bought the museum—to catch the spirit of the thing, you understand."

"We don't understand!" Joe countered. "That

old fellow over there . . ." The boy turned. The chair by the doorway was empty.

"What fellow?" Professor Randolph asked.

Chet's eyes popped. He edged toward the door as the Hardys protested leaving so soon.

"You haven't any right on private property!" roared the man suddenly. "Get out!"

CHAPTER VI

A Peculiar Professor

FRANK and Joe exchanged glances. Perhaps Professor Randolph really had bought the museum!

"I think we'd better play safe and leave," Frank whispered to his brother. "If he's the owner, we're breaking the law by trespassing."

"So gratifying to see you agree with me." The man smirked as the boys walked out. "You realize the cause of education must be served!" He bowed stiffly.

"What a character!" Frank remarked as the three boys stepped into their car. "He reminds me of a comic-strip villain."

Chet bobbed his head to mimic a bow. "To be sure, my dear boys. It's all for education. What do you suppose he teaches?"

Joe grinned. "Young boys, and knows how to put them in their places."

"Perhaps General Smith is acquainted with

Professor Randolph," Frank suggested as they drove through Centerville. "If they're friends, then Randolph will let us in after all."

Soon they reached the house. When the boys entered, they realized the general was battling with a problem of his own. He seemed decidedly agitated and was pacing up and down the living room, his red hair rumpled.

Frank was alarmed. What dire turn of events had occurred? "General Smith, what's the matter?" he asked.

Aroused from his thoughts, the man turned with a start. "Matter? Everything! The house has been ransacked!"

"Good night!" Joe exclaimed. "Since we ate lunch?"

"It must have happened before then," the officer replied. "Nothing downstairs was touched. Just the second-floor bedrooms!"

"None of us went up there at noontime," Frank recalled. "Was anything taken?"

"Nothing of mine so far as I can make out," the officer replied. "The things in our suitcases and dresser drawers were strewn about. You'd better check on your own belongings!"

Frank and Joe ran up the stairs three at a time, and Chet was not far behind. They found their room a picture of disarray. Clothes which had hung in the closet lay on the floor and the contents of their bags were scattered over the rug.

"Gosh," Chet moaned as he began to pick up his things, "I hope they didn't take it."

"Take what?" Joe was curious.

"I had a box of special attachments for my camera in this . . . Oh, here it is!"

The Hardys went on checking their belongings minutely while General Smith watched.

"All my stuff is here," Joe said finally.

"Mine too," Frank added, rising from his kneeling position. Then he let out a sudden exclamation. "Wait! The picture is gone!"

"Picture?" the officer repeated.

"The half-man that Chet snapped in Bayport."

"That proves it!" Joe shouted. "Bush or a cohort has been here! Nobody else would want that photo."

"Right," Frank agreed. "But I don't think that's what he was after. He probably didn't even realize that Chet had taken the snapshot."

"It doesn't matter," Chet piped up. "I have the negative, and I even brought another print in my wallet."

"That's good," Frank continued. "But I'll bet Bush was after a map showing where the lost gold was buried."

"But we haven't any map," Chet replied, perplexed.

"Bush probably thinks we have," Joe said. "Which indicates he still doesn't know where to look for the treasure."

By the time the boys had straightened up the place, General Smith had regained his composure.

"We must get someone to guard this house when we're away," he said. "I know just the man for the job, if he's still in town. I'll send a note to Claude."

General Smith explained to his visitors that Claude was his Army orderly and was on vacation at his home in Centerville, too. The officer requested the boys to deliver the note, as he did not want to leave the house unoccupied. He suggested they continue their sleuthing alone.

Before going, Frank asked General Smith if he knew Professor Randolph, and told him about the incident at the museum.

"No, never heard of him," the general replied. "But it doesn't surprise me that the museum's been sold. It always ran at a loss."

Upon reaching Centerville, Frank parked in the town square. Joe offered to deliver the general's note and started down the narrow, cobblestoned street where the orderly lived. As the others waited for him, Frank gazed across the square. His eyes lighted on the courthouse and an idea occurred to him. If Professor Randolph had bought the museum, the deed would be registered there.

"Wait here a minute," he said to Chet. "I'll be right back."

The courthouse was a low brick building that looked like a church without a steeple. Two heavy white columns stood on either side of the front doorway. Frank entered and asked an attendant where deeds were registered. He was directed to an office down the hall. In it was an old man, beside whose desk towered row upon row of thick volumes of records.

"Something I can do for you?" he asked.

"Yes," Frank replied. "I've been told the old Rocky Run Museum has been sold to a Professor Randolph."

"Hm!" said the man, peering over his spectacles. "That's news to me. Nothing of the sort has been registered here."

"Maybe the deed was recorded while you were out," Frank suggested.

The man hooked his thumbs into his suspenders and tilted back in his chair.

"Son," he said, "I've been settin' here for forty years, 'cept for lunch, and when I'm out this office is closed."

Frank smiled, thanked the man, and walked back to the car. "I had a hunch Professor Randolph's story was a fake," he told Chet and his brother, who had returned from the orderly's house.

"Well," Chet said, "if Randolph is still there, I think that old museum is a good place to stay away from."

"I should say not!" Frank's jaw jutted with determination. "We're going right back and tell Randolph the place isn't his."

"Agreed," said Joe. "And we're going to find out if Randolph has anything to do with our case."

"Say, fellows," Frank whispered, "I think somebody's been watching us." He glanced in the direction of the hotel.

"Who?" Chet asked.

"I didn't see enough to identify him, but I saw a man slip into the alley alongside the building."

Joe looked across the square. Nobody was in sight.

"I don't like this," Frank said uneasily. "I think maybe we had better try a back route to the museum."

"A good idea," Joe agreed. "If anybody's following us, we may throw him off the track this time. Let's go!"

A sandy road led the boys off the main highway and through a stretch of woodland. The trees interlaced high overhead, making a canopy which filtered out the afternoon sun.

"We're not going to get there in a hurry," Joe said. "This road's too bumpy."

Frank deftly steered the car along the rutty road, avoiding large rocks which now and then jutted from the side. They drove down a little gully, then up a steep slope.

"Hey, wait!" Chet shouted suddenly.

"What's up?" Joe asked.

"Look at those deer! I want to get a picture!"

A hundred yards to the left near a brook in the woods stood three deer.

"Okay," Frank said, bringing the car to a halt. "But make it snappy."

Chet climbed out. He flipped open his camera case, then tiptoed into the woods. The deer, being downwind, did not scent the boys. They went on feeding.

"Take them from there," Joe called softly.

"Can't—I have to get closer."

Chet walked a dozen paces, peered into his view finder, and advanced a few more feet.

In the stillness Frank thought he heard the sound of a motor behind them. He looked back. No car was in sight, and the hum stopped.

"Guess I'm jittery," he told himself.

"Hurry up!" Joe motioned to Chet.

But Chet, thinking he could get an even closer shot, continued to advance, tiptoeing as he went. He dropped down on one knee, holding the camera close to his eye. The deer were in perfect range.

But before Chet could click the shutter, a startled shout broke the stillness of the woodland. In a flash the deer leaped away.

Chet whirled about to see who had spoiled his

picture. No one was in sight. In sudden panic he raced back to the road.

"Frank! Joe!" he shouted. "Hey, fellows, where are you?"

No answer came. The car was deserted!

CHAPTER VII

The Search

CHET peered into the car, then stooped to his knees to look underneath it. The Hardys had apparently vanished into thin air!

"Hey, Frank! Joe!" Chet shouted in alarm. Beads of perspiration began to trickle down his freckled face. Again he shouted for his companions. The air was still.

After half an hour of futile waiting and calling for the brothers, Chet was thoroughly alarmed.

He got into the car, turned it around, and started back to Centerville as fast as the rugged road would permit. Finally it joined the main highway and Chet sped through Centerville to the general's house.

"Frank and Joe—they're gone!" he cried out, running into the house.

As Chet related his story, a look of growing concern appeared on the general's face.

"They wouldn't go off without telling me," Chet said breathlessly. "Something's happened to them!"

The general had no doubt of this. "There's not a minute to lose. If we can't locate them ourselves, I'll notify the police."

They got into the car. With General Smith behind the wheel, they pulled away from the house and onto the main highway.

Soon they came to the intersection where the boys had left the highway. The officer took the bumpy road which led into the woods.

"Where does this go?" Chet asked.

"It stays straight for a mile, then makes a complete loop and comes out near the old Beauregard Smith plantation."

"Jumpin' catfish!" Chet exclaimed. "Then we were going in the wrong direction for the museum anyway!"

It was not long before the convertible dipped into the gully and rose over the brow of the hill where Frank had stopped for Chet's attempted photo of the deer.

"Here's the place!" Chet said.

Braking to a halt and shutting off the motor, General Smith stepped out. Chet followed.

"There must have been a struggle here," the officer said, examining scuff marks in front of a dense thicket.

"The trail leads this way." Chet pointed to

dragging heel marks. "Frank and Joe must have been kidnapped!"

With Chet following, the general pushed into the underbrush and advanced into the dank woodland. Ferns and tiny white wild flowers which carpeted the forest had been trampled. The route was clear, and the officer was making swift progress.

The man pressed on relentlessly, unmindful of the briers that tore his trousers, and seemingly unaware that Chet was puffing along behind him like a heavy tank.

But dusk was falling rapidly, and soon the gloom was so dense that further progress was impossible without a light.

"What a dud I am!" the general exclaimed. "Coming off like this without a flashlight!"

Chet, more eager than ever to find his friends, volunteered to return to the convertible for a flashlight. A short time later, perspiring heavily, he was back with the light.

"Here you are, sir."

"Good work."

They set off again, this time at a snail's pace, in order not to miss any telltale heel marks made by one of the kidnapped boys. An hour passed as they continued combing through brush.

"I haven't seen any tracks for a hundred yards," said the general, stopping to take stock of the situation.

"Do you suppose the kidnappers went down the stream?" Chet asked.

"Very possibly. They may have waded a distance to throw us off their trail."

The searchers combed the pasture grass to the edge of the stream, but not a clue came to light. Discouraged, and completely tired out after the long search, both lay down to rest. To add to their discomfort, it began to rain. The rain came down so hard that they crossed the stream and took shelter under some overhanging rocks.

The rain continued all night as Chet and the general slept fitfully on improvised beds of leaves. A faint streak of light had brushed the eastern horizon before the torrent stopped. Now the hunt could be resumed in daylight.

The man and boy rose wearily and stretched their cramped limbs.

"I sure could use some breakfast!" Chet muttered sadly.

"Or a dry, comfortable bed!" the general added ruefully. "But we'd better get moving if we're going to find Frank and Joe."

"I hope the kidnappers haven't taken them far. I'll look on this side of Rocky Run for footprints," Chet offered.

"Very good," General Smith agreed. "The boys may have crossed somewhere."

Chet zigzagged along the bank.

"See anything?" called the officer, who was searching in the opposite direction.

Chet shook his head in the negative, then suddenly let out a whoop. He held up a shoe!

General Smith hurried to the boy's side.

Impressed into the lining were the words *Peck Co. Bayport*.

"Nice work! Come on!"

Once more they probed the grass.

"Here's the trail again," said the general, following patches of recently broken vegetation over the hill.

"Golly, what a climb!" Chet puffed.

Grasping scrubby trees on the hillside, the man and boy worked their way to the top of the incline. The bare rocks there revealed no clue of recent travelers, nor had the mossy slope down the other side been disturbed lately by any human foot.

Slipping over the steep rocks, Chet and the general descended the hill again to the spot where the shoe had been found.

They moved ahead slowly, examining every bent tuft of grass. Suddenly Chet stopped.

"Come here, General Smith!" he called excitedly.

"What's up?"

Chet did not answer. He stood spellbound.

"Listen!"

The officer obeyed. At first he could hear only

the ripple of the brook and the clear whistle of an oriole.

"Nothing unusual."

"Shh! It may come again."

The general strained to catch the faintest sound.

Then it came to him. A muffled shout from somewhere down inside the earth!

CHAPTER VIII

An Important Lead

"SOMEBODY's under these rocks," Chet shouted. He rushed forward, his hands pulling at the vines which blanketed several boulders. "General Smith, look what's here!"

By the time the officer arrived at the boy's side, Chet had uncovered an old wooden door fitted into the face of a big rock. Its rusted hinges were fastened to the boulder with long iron spikes. A rotting leather thong served as a doorknob.

"Frank! Joe!" The general leaned close to the door and shouted. There was a muffled answer.

"We'll get you out!" Chet called.

He took hold of the leather thong, which broke at his pull. "We'll have to pry the door open," he said.

"Let me get hold of it," General Smith offered.

The husky man picked up a sharp stone and banged out an old knot in the wood, making room for two of his fingers. With a mighty grunt he pulled on the door. It creaked, then suddenly yawned open.

A whiff of stagnant air, redolent of rotting wood and sour earth, burst forth. Chet and the general peered inside the dark hole.

The sound of stifled voices came from the rear of the cave. The general pulled out the flashlight and clicked it on. The glow fell on two figures, lying on the dank ground. They were tied and gagged.

"Frank!" Chet shouted. "Joe!"

Quickly he and the officer removed the gags from the boys' mouths and unfastened their bindings.

"Oh-h!" Joe said, rising and stretching his cramped legs. "We thought you'd never find us."

Frank rubbed his arms briskly to restore the circulation. "Gosh, are we glad to see you!"

"What happened?" General Smith asked, as soon as he was assured that the Hardys had not been injured.

"While Joe and I were waiting for Chet to get a picture of the deer," Frank said, "three men jumped us. We were gagged and blindfolded. They must have followed us from Centerville."

"Who were they?" Chet asked.

"Couldn't tell," Joe replied. "They wore masks. But listen to this. *One of them was called Junior!*"

"Probably very young," General Smith cried out. "Could be one of the men who tried to kidnap me from your house!"

"I'm sure this was the same person," Frank said.

"And I didn't see a thing happen!" Chet moaned.

"Go on with your story," urged the officer. "This must be reported—kidnapping is a Federal offense."

"They marched us through the woods," Joe explained. "Since our hands were tied, we couldn't drop anything to leave a trail for you to find."

"So you did the next best thing," remarked the general. "You made marks with your feet."

Joe smiled. "That was Frank's idea. Every once in a while he'd drag one of his feet as if he were stumbling."

"Good headwork!" the general said admiringly. "It's lucky Chet decided to look on the other side of the brook. That's where he found the shoe."

Joe explained that the lace had become loose as he stumbled along, and the shoe had fallen off.

"A break for you!" General Smith exclaimed. "Your shoe led us to this place. Here, put it on."

As Joe tied the lace, Chet asked, "What kind of place is this? Feels like a tomb."

"It's an old smokehouse," Frank replied. "Guess it hasn't been used for years." He shuddered. "Let's get out in the sun so we can dry out."

The clear, warm air of the early morning sent a glow through Frank and Joe as they made their way back to the car and rode to the general's home. There the front door was opened by a middle-aged Negro, beaming broadly. His courteous welcome reminded the boys of the gentle traditions of the Old South.

"Good morning, General."

"Right on the job, Claude. I knew I could depend on you."

After introducing his three guests, the general ordered breakfast. This gave the boys time for a couple of phone calls.

Frank got in touch with the local police chief, told him about the kidnapping, and asked if there was any criminal known locally as Junior. The chief searched his files and reported that to his knowledge there was not. He added that he would send out a bulletin on the kidnappers.

Next, Frank called Bayport. A few seconds later Aunt Gertrude answered. When Frank asked for his father, his aunt said he had not returned yet from Washington. Then she added apprehensively:

"Something serious must be happening, Frank, or you wouldn't be calling home."

"You're right," he admitted. "We've run into a character named Junior. I thought Dad could check his files for a criminal by that name."

"Junior!" The detective's sister grasped the import at once. "One of the men who tried to break into our house! He's chasing you down South?"

"He was, Auntie. Now we're chasing him."

"Well, look out for him! He's a wolf in sheep's clothing. I'll tell your father about Junior. You're running up a big telephone bill. Good-by."

Grinning, Frank hung up when he heard a click on the other end of the line.

Presently Claude announced, "Breakfast is served!"

With those welcome words, the boys and the general sat down to an old-fashioned Southern repast. Chet's face was aglow as Claude served chilled cantaloupe, followed by crisp-fringed pancakes and broiled ham. Then he brought in a platter of fried eggs, a dish of raspberry jam, and piping hot muffins.

Letting his belt out a notch, Chet asked, "General, does everybody eat like this in the South?"

"They used to," the officer replied, smiling. "Most people are in too much of a hurry today to enjoy the art of good cooking."

"Not me!" Chet decorated another muffin with a daub of jam. "The South's a wonderful place, General."

"Now let's go back to the museum," Joe said when they finished eating.

"We've already paid our admission without a chance to look around," Chet put in. "We ought to get in free today!"

General Smith, anxious to get to the police station to talk to the chief about the boys' kidnapping, promised to join them after their visit to the museum.

A short time later the Hardys and Chet arrived at the old farmhouse. When they walked through the front door, a new guard greeted them. In the friendly old Negro's place sat a stout man, whose red face was particularly striking because of a scar that ran from the side of his mouth like an extra-wide smile.

He apparently was wearing the same gray suit, because the front gaped open where the buttons were struggling to hold the jacket together.

"What do you kids want?" the man asked gruffly.

"We've come to look at the exhibits," Frank replied.

"The museum's closed."

"No, it's not!" Joe shot back. "Where'd that old man go?"

"The professor will tell you!" growled the man. "Professor!"

Randolph suddenly appeared from behind a glass display case. "Back again, eh?"

"We're going to finish the tour you interrupted yesterday," Frank stated firmly.

"I repeat," the professor intoned, his voice rising in a crescendo, "this place now belongs to me!"

"There's no deed recorded in your name at the courthouse!" Frank said evenly.

The man winced, then he said with a curl to his lips, "They haven't had time to file one yet. I bought the place only yesterday." Suddenly he became more friendly. "Well, Smi—" He caught himself as he looked at the guard, "I guess we can let 'em look around. But this is the last time, boys.

"Keep an eye on things," he told his man, "till I get the deed recorded." With that, he stalked out the front door.

Frank, Joe, and Chet browsed around the museum. A case full of old sabers intrigued Joe, who examined the ornate handles and noted the keen edges of the blades.

"Hey, look! An old mess kit," Chet exclaimed.

"Always thinking about food," Frank quipped, stepping over to see the odd collection of utensils. "Hey, what are you chewing on now?"

"Gum. Want a piece?"

"No thanks."

Joe picked up a battered pewter pan. "This looks as if it had been creased by a bullet."

"Here's an old canteen," Frank observed.

He held the metal water bottle in his hand, turning it over and over. Its cloth covering had long since rotted off, but the two rings remained where a strap once had held it over a trooper's shoulder.

Frank unscrewed the top and peered inside. "There's something in the bottom of this," he whispered to Joe.

His brother put an eye to the small opening. "You're right. Looks like a bit of paper." Joe turned the canteen over and shook it vigorously, but failed to dislodge the paper.

"Wait a sec. I've got an idea," Frank said. "Chet, lend me your chewing gum."

"But it's unsanitary. I'll give—"

"Hand it over!" Chet obeyed as Frank pulled a pencil from his pocket. He pressed the sticky gum to the end of the yellow stick, inserted it in the canteen, and made contact with the paper. *Out it came!*

"You're a genius, Frank," Chet said admiringly.

Just then the museum guard leaned far back in his creaking chair. Frank caught the movement out of the corner of his eye.

"He's trying to watch us," the boy warned. "Let's go over to the other side of the room."

Frank put the old canteen down where he had found it and walked to the front of the fireplace, Joe and Chet following. Then, very carefully, Frank opened the paper.

As the boys waited intently, Frank's eyes almost popped. "Listen to this!" In guarded tones he read aloud the short message:

" *'Dying. Can't make it back. Got General*

Smith's bandoleer. May be war secret. Hid it in Pleasanton's Bridge when chase hot.

Bing'"

Joe gave a low whistle. "This must have been written by Charles Bingham, the spy suspected of stealing the bandoleer!"

Frank quickly folded the note.

"Let's go find that bridge!"

CHAPTER IX

A Trap

THE boys decided to take the Civil War message to General Smith. Frank tucked it into his wallet, and made for the door. As he, Joe, and Chet left, the guard called after them in a gravelly voice:

"Remind yourselves not to come back!"

The boys paid no attention. After waiting a moment for Chet to snap a picture of the historical building in which the important clue had been found, Frank drove toward Centerville. Stopping in front of a service station, he asked for gas and requested directions to Pleasanton's Bridge.

"Pleasanton's Bridge? Never heard of it," replied the attendant.

"It's in the vicinity of Rocky Run," Frank said, "or at least it ought to be."

"I've lived here a long time," declared the man as he wiped the windshield, "but I sure never heard of a Pleasanton's Bridge."

"More bad luck," Joe remarked as they drove off. "Now that we've found a good clue, we can't locate the bridge."

The boys' next call was at Centerville's one-room library. Frank asked the pleasant, gray-haired librarian for a book on local Civil War history.

"Thanks very much," Frank said, taking several books which the woman suggested. "Perhaps you can help us find what we're looking for."

When he told of their quest for Pleasanton's Bridge, the librarian took off her spectacles and frowned in deep thought.

"A Captain Pleasanton was in the Battle of Rocky Run," she stated. "But I've never heard of a bridge by that name."

Sitting down with the boys, she helped them scan the books, in a vain search for the mysterious bridge. When their perusal proved to be of no avail, Frank thanked the woman for her help.

Chet smiled wryly as the boys left the library. "Well, fellows, I guess the mystery of the lost gold ends right here," he sighed. "There's not much we can do now."

Frank set his jaw and snapped his fingers. "Wait! I have it!"

"What?" Chet asked as he and Joe followed Frank at a brisk jog across the square.

Frank headed for the courthouse. Joe kept pace,

but their stout friend lagged behind, his eye on a luncheonette and candy store.

The Hardys went straight to the old man who registered deeds. He recognized Frank at once.

"Lookin' up more deeds?" he asked.

"No," Frank said with a smile. "I'm looking for a bridge. Pleasanton's Bridge."

Frank's pulse quickened at the registrar's sudden look of understanding. "Pleasanton's Bridge! Well, son, I hadn't heard mention of that in many a year, until just a little while ago."

"What do you mean?" Frank asked apprehensively.

"You're the second fellow to ask me that question in less than an hour," the man said. "Y'all playing a game?"

Frank assured him they were not, and asked what the other inquirer looked like.

"He was a tall, dark man. Stranger to me. Didn't give his name."

"Did he have a mustache?" Joe asked, suspecting Professor Randolph at once.

"No. Clean-shaven."

The Hardys were puzzled. Was the stranger Dr. Bush?

"Did you tell the man where the bridge is?" Frank asked, trying hard to conceal his excitement.

The registrar took a deep puff on his pipe and blew a cloud of smoke into the air.

"Take it easy, son. Nothing to get wrought up about. The bridge isn't there any more."

"It's gone?" Joe asked.

The old man ran his thumbs up and down his suspenders and leaned back in his chair. Then, with measured words, he told them that Pleasanton's was the military name given a stone and timber bridge over Rocky Run. It was called this because a Captain Pleasanton had been assigned to defend it. A furious battle had raged on either side of the span, and when Pleasanton had found his position untenable, he had destroyed the bridge.

"Then there's nothing left of it?" Joe asked.

"Wouldn't say that. The old abutments are still standing," the man replied, drawing the flame of a match into the bowl of his corncob pipe. "I'll tell y'all how to find it. Go south on the county road two miles and turn right till you come to the new bridge over Rocky Run. Pleasanton's Bridge is 'bout half a mile downstream."

The boys thanked the old man and hurried out. As they got into their car, Chet arrived with a large bag of sandwiches and three cartons of milk.

"Guess this'll do for lunch," he said with a grin.

"More'n that," Frank said. "Hop in. We're bound for Pleasanton's Bridge."

"You found out where it is?" Chet asked increduously. Then he pointed to a poster on a telegraph pole at the curb. " 'Civil War Rifle Shoot on the twenty-third,' " the boy read. "That's tomorrow, fellows. I'd like to see it!"

"Sounds like fun," Joe agreed.

Frank drove down the highway and turned off where the registrar had told him. He pulled up at the new bridge.

"Say, this is the place where the guy in the black sedan stopped to look at us," Chet remarked. "Hope he isn't around here now."

"We'll keep our eyes open," Frank promised.

The boys realized it would be necessary to walk from this spot to the site of Pleasanton's Bridge, since Rocky Run left the road here and meandered through the fields and woods.

Frank drove the car behind a clump of trees. After eating their picnic lunch, the three boys started downstream to find Pleasanton's Bridge. They followed the faint trace of a long-forgotten trail beside the water.

"This stream must be on the Beauregard Smith plantation," Joe remarked as they went along.

Warily the three pushed on, searching for a sign of the old bridge. Suddenly at the base of a little rise they came upon a pile of rotted logs.

"An old cabin," Chet said. "Maybe Pleasanton's Bridge was a toll bridge, and the bridge tender lived here."

The boys walked around the perimeter of the

ruins. Frank pointed to broken bits of dishes and a crushed rusted kettle buried beneath one of the logs.

"Guess this is all that's left of the place, and I don't see any sign of a bridge."

Suddenly Chet gave a whoop. "Oh boy! A Civil War rifle!"

Some twenty feet ahead lay an antique firing piece, its barrel glinting in the sun. Chet rushed toward it.

But Frank's sharp warning stayed his friend's quick motion. "Don't touch that thing!"

Chet's hand was barely six inches from the rifle when he pulled it back.

"This may be a trap!" Frank warned. "That weapon's too shiny to have been here long."

The older Hardy walked swiftly into the thicket and ripped a twining vine from an old stump. Tying several pieces together, Frank made a long string from the tendrils. Carefully, and without touching the rifle, he tied one end to the stock.

Then Frank motioned Joe and Chet to stand off at some distance behind a tree. When all three boys were concealed, Frank tugged gently on the other end of the vine.

Into the air flew a shower of sparks!

"Good night!" Chet cried. "The rifle's charged with electricity!"

"This may be a trap!" Frank warned

"I thought there was something phony about it," Frank said grimly.

He tugged on the vine again. Another arc of sparks flew from the weapon, hissing and crackling.

"I—I think we'd better get out of here fast!" Chet declared, moving back.

Suddenly the sparks stopped. Frank felt a gentle release on the rifle as if it had loosened from something. He pulled the weapon toward him.

"What do you suppose charged it?" Chet wondered, wide-eyed, when the old firing piece finally lay at their feet.

The boys cautiously examined the spot where the weapon had lain. As they probed the grass with sticks, Joe pointed out a long wire.

"This must have been attached to the rifle!" he exclaimed. "Let's see where it goes!"

Knowing that the wire probably was still charged, the three poked along its course with meticulous care.

Just beyond, the sight that greeted the boys made them shudder. On the other side of the trees was an electric power line. And looped over one of the cables was the wire they were following!

"Bush's men, or somebody, apparently will stop at nothing!" Frank exclaimed. "That trap was laid with professional skill."

Standing far back from the wire, he knocked it from the overhead cable with a stick. It hit the ground, rendered harmless to anyone else who might pass by.

"This proves one thing to me," Frank declared. "Pleasanton's Bridge must be near here. Come on. Let's find it!"

Just as Chet and the Hardys started out, a flash of lightning streaked the sky, followed by a deep roll of thunder. In a minute it grew as dark as night. A moment later a torrent of rain whipped the woodland furiously, accompanied by a heavy wind which tore through the treetops. Rocky Run was almost obscured by the downpour.

The boys ducked under some low bushes, hoping the storm would subside. Instead, it grew worse. Lightning traced jagged patterns in the black sky and thunder roared through the hills.

"We'd better go back!" Chet shouted. "It's not . . ."

A blinding flash, coming simultaneously with a terrible ripping sound, interrupted the boy.

"Watch out!"

Joe pitched himself at Chet, bowling him out of the way of the splintered trunk of a tree only an instant before it buried itself in the brush where the boy had been crouching.

"That was too close for comfort!" Chet panted with fright. "Let's get out of these woods!"

The Hardys needed no urging. With Joe carrying the rifle, the boys quickly made their way through the howling, thrashing storm. They were drenched and water was squishing out of their shoes by the time they reached the car and tumbled onto the seats. Frank quickly started the engine and headed through the teeming rain toward Centerville.

Reaching General Smith's home, the soaked boys dashed to their rooms for a change of clothes. Upon returning to the first floor, they found their host in the living room. The man was greatly agitated when he heard the story of the electrified trap.

"An attempt to kill you! I'd like to lay my hands on those fiends! Where's the rifle?"

"On the back seat of the car," Joe said. "I'll go out and get it."

"No, wait till it stops pouring."

Then the boys related the episode of finding the note in the canteen and showed it to the general. He was astonished.

"This is remarkable!" the officer exclaimed incredulously. "Now we're ready for the big push! And I'd suggest no time be lost."

"I think the rifle may prove to be a good clue, too," Frank declared. He glanced out the window. "It's stopped raining now. I'll go get it."

Side-stepping puddles of water like a football player in broken-field practice, he ran to the garage.

"What's this?" Frank said, stepping inside. He

bent down to examine wet footprints on one side of the car.

"Oh no!" An awful thought flashed through his mind. Frank put his hand on the car door handle. *Wet!* The boy's fears were confirmed when he flung the door open.

Inside the house, Joe and the general waited for Frank to return with the gun clue. They heard his racing steps, then saw him dash into the room empty-handed.

"Where's the rifle?" Joe said.

"It's gone!"

"Impossible!"

"I tell you, Joe, the rifle's disappeared!"

CHAPTER X

The Missing Rifle

"I CAN'T believe it!" Joe dashed out to search for himself. Soon it was obvious to all of them—the rifle had disappeared.

"We were followed!" Frank exclaimed. "What chumps we were not to bring it into the house!"

"Somebody must have wanted that gun pretty badly to come out in the storm to get it," Chet commented when they were in the house again.

"It was probably covered with the culprit's fingerprints," Frank mused. "Anyway, there goes a piece of evidence."

Joe thought a moment. "Maybe someone plans to use it in the shoot tomorrow. We'll have to do some investigating there."

"You're a good marksman, Joe," Chet spoke up. "Why don't you enter the contest?"

"With what?" Joe asked.

General Smith got up, walked over to a cabinet,

and unlocked it. "Here's my great-grandfather's rifle," he said. "Glad to have you use it, Joe."

The boy was thrilled and gratefully accepted the offer. That evening, after a sumptuous Southern dinner expertly prepared by Claude, the general schooled the boys in the nomenclature of Civil War firearms and gave Joe pointers on firing.

"These old muzzle loaders," the officer said, "fired homemade bullets. I have a box of them you can use tomorrow." He produced the bullets and also a mold in which they were made.

The three boys could hardly wait until the next morning, which dawned bright and clear, an ideal day for a rifle shoot.

Claude served another delicious breakfast, which included hot biscuits and a fluffy omelet. Then, taking the general's antique rifle, the boys and the officer drove to the site of the marksmanship event. The target range was laid out at the edge of town in a field alongside the highway.

Joe registered with the officials, who examined his weapon and approved it. Then he joined his companions, and all walked up to the firing line. On a table lay the prizes. The one marked first prize took the boys' eyes. It was the latest model target rifle with a telescopic sight.

Suddenly Joe clutched Frank's arm. "There's the stolen rifle!" He pointed to a youth holding an antique firing piece.

The Hardys spoke quietly to the others, doing their best to conceal the excitement they felt.

"This is the time for a showdown!" Joe declared.

"I agree," the officer assented.

"We'd better confront him right now before the meet begins," Frank suggested.

With the general following, the boys strode over to where the youth was standing. Joe faced him squarely.

"I believe that's my rifle you have."

"Says who?" The youth stared defiantly as a small crowd gathered, sensing a fracas.

"We all say so!" Frank said firmly.

The youth raised the weapon menacingly.

"Prove it!" he cried.

"Put that down!" General Smith snapped.

The officer's command, plus the added weight of his uniform, caused the young fellow to change his attitude. He lowered the rifle until the stock rested on the ground, then continued his protest.

"I didn't take nobody's gun," he said stoutly. "You can't prove this is yours."

Joe realized that he had only a slim claim to the rifle. Since he had found the weapon in the woods, he could present no receipt to show he had purchased it. The boy might be telling the truth. There was the possibility that two firing pieces were identical.

General Smith broke the deadlock. "We'll look

into this later. The shoot mustn't be delayed."

At that moment an official sounded the bugle call. The contestants lined up. The shoot began with burst after burst of musketry.

As Frank watched Joe with his shirt open at the neck and his eye cocked over the sight of the Civil War rifle, he mused that his brother could have stepped out of the pages of a history book!

The boy's finely muscled arms held the weapon firmly and the general observed with pleasure his gentle squeeze of the trigger.

"Atta boy, Joe!" Chet shouted as his friend scored a bull's-eye.

Joe gave his companions a brief smile, then hurried to reload. The boy handled the firearm like a veteran, blazing away shot after shot.

"Cease fire!"

As one of the judges shouted the command, the riflemen put down their weapons so the targets could be inspected. The four with the highest scores would continue.

Joe turned out to be among the remaining contestants—and so was the youth he had confronted!

"Come on, Joe, beat that guy!" Chet banged a clenched fist into the palm of his hand.

Joe looked toward the general. The officer nodded encouragingly as the meet resumed. Ten shots apiece!

Joe's rifle spoke with precision as he sent bullet

after bullet ripping into the target. Once Joe glanced at the youth standing beside him. His opponent remained calm and expressionless, firing quickly after loading and aiming.

A sudden silence told the onlookers the marksmen had finished. The judges hurried forward to examine the targets.

"Five out of ten!" one of them reported, peering at the first target.

"Seven out of ten!" came the next call.

The official who examined the surly youth's target announced, "Eight out of ten!"

A judge studied Joe's target. The man paused a moment and beckoned another official to his side. Together they examined the card carefully. One of them cleared his throat.

"Eight out of ten! Tie score!"

Frank ran up and thumped his brother on the back. "Swell, Joe!"

The boy grinned. "But I didn't win." He stepped toward the fellow who had tied the score. "Nice going! Maybe they'll let us shoot it out." His rival turned on his heel and walked away.

"Great guy!" Chet muttered sarcastically.

General Smith praised Joe and went on to say that the judges were arranging a shoot-off.

"You'll get a ten-minute rest," he relayed. "Sit down here on the grass and relax."

As Joe stretched out beside his rifle, Frank and Chet wandered off among the spectators.

"Let's see if we can find Joe's rival," Frank suggested. Then he added, "Oh, hi there!"

"Enjoyin' yourself?" asked the genial old Registrar of Deeds from the courthouse.

"We sure are!" Frank answered. "It's great fun to watch them shoot these old Civil War weapons."

"They made some real dandy guns in the old days," the man mused. "My grandfather manufactured 'em. But I don't know what's becomin' of our local boys," he added regretfully.

"What do you mean?"

The old man took a couple of quick puffs at his corncob pipe and blew the smoke idly out of the corner of his mouth.

"Our boys," he said, "ain't as good shots as you visitin' fellers."

"But one of your local fellows tied my brother! And who knows—he might win the meet," Frank observed.

"You mean that lad with the steady eye? He ain't from these parts," the man declared.

The remark startled Frank. "You mean he's a visitor, too? He talks like you folks in Centerville."

"Don't know where he's from, but it ain't Centerville," the man insisted.

Just then Chet, who had been standing nearby looking at the crowd, pulled Frank's arm. "Come here quick."

"What's up?"

"That guy over there. Whoops—he's gone now!"

"Who was he?"

" 'Smi—' something, that scar-mouthed guy at the museum. He was standing right behind you when you were talking to that old fellow. I bet he was trying to hear what you said."

Frank scanned the crowd, but could see no figure resembling Professor Randolph's guard.

Disappointed, Frank turned to Chet. "I have some interesting news. Let's go back to Joe."

They hurried to where Joe was reclining. General Smith was sitting on a tree stump alongside of him.

Frank told them about his brother's rival not being a local inhabitant. "The whole setup seems odd," he remarked. "I'd say he bears some investigating."

"Perhaps he's one of the 'strangers' my friend Jeb was talking about," General Smith commented, frowning.

"I'm going to ask him where he's from," Frank said. He strolled off in the direction of the youth who had reappeared, and was standing alone under a tree.

Chet followed eagerly.

"Good shooting!" Frank declared, walking up to the young man. The Hardy boy received only a cold stare.

"I hear you're not from town," Frank went on pleasantly. "Where do you hail from?"

"What business is it of yours?"

"Just curious," Frank replied nonchalantly.

Suddenly the youth's expression hardened. A frown creased his forehead, making him look much older. His eyes darted through the crowd as if he were looking for someone.

Frank's eyes followed. Perhaps the marksman was seeking a pal, the young sleuth mused.

As the Hardy boy diverted his gaze to the crowd, the wily youth swung the barrel of his rifle.

"Duck!" Chet shouted. But not in time.

The weapon caught Frank on the side of the head and he fell dizzily to the ground!

CHAPTER XI

Pleasanton's Bridge

A SHOUT went up from the onlookers at the shoot.
Chet tried to grab Frank's assailant, but the fellow
gave him a quick shove which sent the stout boy
sprawling. Then the stranger whirled and darted
along the fringes of the crowd.

In a second Frank staggered to his feet. Despite
the pain from the blow to his head, he set off after
his adversary. Chet raced behind.

Joe, who had been attracted by the noise of the
crowd, joined the chase.

As the attacker ran into the woods, Frank was
hot on his trail. Suddenly a voice like chilled steel
rang out.

"Stop where you are!"

A long rifle barrel protruded from behind a
tree. Frank immediately recognized it as that of
the youth.

In a flash Frank hurled himself to the ground, behind a bush. As he lay there, wondering what he should do next, the ambusher uttered a cry of pain. The weapon dropped from his grasp. Then the rifleman turned and dashed off through the brush like a streak of lightning.

"Are you all right, Frank?" came a voice behind him.

Frank rolled over to see his brother looking down at him anxiously.

"Did you do that?" Frank asked as he rose from the ground.

"Sure did. When I saw you drop, I figured something must be the matter. Then I spotted the rifle barrel sticking out from behind the tree, so I grabbed a rock and threw at it. Pretty good pitching if I do say so myself."

"Glad you didn't miss," Frank remarked wryly, advancing with Joe toward the place where the weapon had fallen. "You probably saved my life!"

Frank picked up the rifle and the two boys returned to where they had left General Smith.

Enraged by the story of the unwarranted attack on Frank, the general immediately went to find an official to report the incident.

"Did you find out that guy's name?" Frank asked his brother as they examined the firing piece.

"No. But maybe the general did. Here he comes now."

General Smith hurried up with the judges of the meet. With them was a policeman. Joe told of the ambush incident.

"That kid won't get away with this," the policeman declared. "I'll report it right away."

Joe asked who the boy was.

The general answered. "He signed the registrar as Jimmy somebody, but he scribbled the last name. We can't make it out.

"Probably done on purpose," Frank remarked. Suddenly he snapped his fingers. "Why didn't I think of it before? I'll bet Jimmy is Junior of Bush's gang! This rifle certainly looks like the one set as a trap in the woods!"

Their conversation was interrupted by the sound of somebody crashing through the bushes. Out burst Chet, his clothes bedraggled and perspiration pouring from his face.

"Where've you been? Running a marathon?" Joe asked his friend, who was gasping for breath.

Frank threw his arm around the boy's shoulders. "Take it easy, Chet. We can wait."

When he was breathing normally again, Chet swallowed hard and said, "I saw him! I know where he went!"

"Who?"

"That guy who socked Frank."

Chet said he had seen the stranger flee, had circled the woods, and spotted the fellow coming out of the trees at the edge of Centerville. He had headed into town, and Chet had followed, unobserved.

"I . . . I saw him run into the hotel," the boy reported. "I peeked in a window, and there he was in the lobby talking to Professor Randolph!"

"Good night!" Joe exploded.

"I wonder what they're up to," Frank mused. "Let's go and find out!"

Leaving the judges, who promised to send Joe the prize rifle which he had won by default, the boys and the general hurried to their car. Joe locked his borrowed rifle, as well as the vengeful youth's weapon, in the trunk. Then, with Frank at the wheel, the group sped to Centerville.

The Hardys dashed through the hotel doorway. Joe, in his headlong rush, bowled over a man onto the plush carpet of the lobby floor.

"Oh, sorry," the boy said, bending over to help the man to his feet. "Professor Randolph!"

The man brushed off his suit coat, straightened his string tie, and glared. "Watch where you're going! Do you want to hurt somebody?"

"We don't," Frank spoke up. "But we have an idea somebody you know would like to harm us."

"Name's Jimmy," Joe blurted. "He nearly took a shot at my brother in the woods! Where is he?"

The professor stepped back a pace, his eyes narrowing as the general entered the lobby with Chet. "I don't know what you're talking about," he said firmly.

"I saw you talking to him right in this lobby!" Chet declared.

The professor's eyes snapped fire. "I don't know anybody named Jimmy," he said icily. "If you'll step aside, I'll continue on my way." He hurried out the door and quickly disappeared.

"Maybe you got your wires crossed, Chet, and saw him talking to somebody else," Joe said.

Chet insisted he was not mistaken. At his suggestion, Frank checked with the desk clerk, who verified that Randolph had been talking to a young man. The clerk's description of the youth fitted Frank's assailant.

The three boys went to the hotel washroom, where Frank bathed the bruise on the side of his head.

"We'll have to go to the museum if we want to get hold of Randolph again," Joe declared as they returned to the hotel porch where General Smith stood waiting.

But Frank thought they should get to Pleasanton's Bridge without delay. The general settled the matter.

"You fellows continue your search for the gold," he said. "I'll go to the museum to investigate this man Randolph." The general grinned. "It'll give me a chance to find out how much I've learned from you Hardys about detective work."

After a quick lunch at the hotel, the boys set off

once more for Pleasanton's Bridge. Frank drove to the new span and parked the car behind a huge old oak tree, hoping no one would notice it.

Presently they reached the pile of rotting logs that once had been a cabin. All was peaceful. Rocky Run gurgled and churned musically around the smooth boulders scattered along the stream bed.

"Let's take a rest," Chet suggested. "This heat is killing me."

Frank remarked it was no place to be caught napping. "The more we keep our eyes open, the better it will be," he said.

The boys went on. About fifteen minutes later, they came upon two stone abutments on either side of the stream. They were completely covered with vines and moss.

"We've found Pleasanton's Bridge!" shouted Joe, running toward the ancient stonework. "Now for the bandoleer!"

Was the clue to the lost gold somewhere within the massive piles of stone and mortar? the boys wondered eagerly. Or had someone already found it?

"We'll have to go over each stone individually," Frank said. "I may as well start on this side of the water." He began work on one part of the abutment.

Chet and Joe decided to cross over to the other

side. They stepped carefully on large rocks and made their way to the opposite bank. The shady coolness of the stream and overhanging trees was a welcome relief to the perspiring boys. They feverishly began to examine each rock and crack in the old structure.

"Guess they built this thing to last a million years," Chet called out as he climbed higher on the pile of stones.

Frank was too busy to reply. His hands felt the rough surface of one stone after another. His knife probed every moss-covered crack between the ancient building blocks.

Occasionally a piece of the abutment would fall into the stream with a loud splash. Frank found a loose section of mortar, and pried away at it. Like a thin wedge of pie, mortar slipped out, leaving just enough room for Frank to slide his hand into the crevice. His middle finger found a small opening in the stone.

"Joe! Chet! Come here!"

"Find something?"

"I think this stone'll come out!" Frank called excitedly. "Help me chip away the rest of the mortar." The two quickly came to his aid.

Using sharp rocks and their pocketknives, the three boys speedily cut away the crumbling cement that held the stones together. Frank tugged at the stone with the hole in it. The stone moved a fraction!

"It's coming!" he shouted.

With a sliding, grinding sound the big stone was yanked from the spot where it had lain, for decades. Quickly Frank peered into the gaping hole.

"I see it!" he cried hoarsely. "The bandoleer!"

CHAPTER XII

The Cap Box

FRANK reached into the hole and pulled out the bandoleer. Its leather strap was rotted with age, and worn away from the rusted buckle. But the silver cap box was still firmly attached by two rivets. While Joe and Chet looked on excitedly, Frank tried to open the box.

"There doesn't seem to be any way to unfasten the lid," he said. "Must be a secret lock on it."

"Let me try it," Joe said eagerly, reaching for the bandoleer.

"Careful," Frank warned. "Don't break the leather. General Smith will certainly want to keep this."

Joe handled the bandoleer gingerly, turning the box over and over in a vain attempt to locate a hasp or tiny hinges.

"I can't find any opening, either," he said

finally. "We'll have to put it under a magnifying glass."

"Let me see it," Chet begged, extending an eager hand.

As Joe gave the bandoleer to his friend, they heard a woman scream. The cry for help that followed came from the woods just ahead!

"Someone's in trouble!" Frank cried.

The three boys raced in the direction from which the sound had come. The Hardys soon outdistanced Chet, who panted some distance behind them.

Joe and Frank searched futilely for the woman who had screamed. "Hello! Hello!" Joe shouted, but got no reply.

"That's funny," Frank said. "The voice sounded as if — Hey, did you hear Chet cry out?"

The Hardys turned and rushed back. A hundred feet beyond, Chet was struggling up from the ground, rubbing his head. His hands were empty!

"G-get him!" he cried hoarsely. "Someone hit me from behind and grabbed the bandoleer!"

The Hardys waited for no further explanation than Chet's pointing finger. The cry had clearly been a hoax to separate the trio while someone stole the secret to the missing gold. Probably the thief had called in a falsetto voice, then had circled back through the brush to waylay Chet.

The boys could hear two persons crashing

through the woodland, and raced after them at top speed.

"They're heading for the highway!" Frank exclaimed.

The brothers saw two figures scramble up the embankment to the new bridge. A moment later they heard the roar of a motor.

"Oh no!" Joe cried in dismay.

The familiar black sedan, which apparently had been parked on the other side of the bridge, sped off in the direction of Centerville.

"We'll catch them!" Frank dashed toward their own car, then let out a cry of despair. The left front tire of the vehicle was flat! "Bush's men must have let the air out!"

"What goofs we were not to leave Chet here on guard while you and I searched for the bandoleer," Joe said bitterly.

At that moment Chet lumbered up the bank and onto the bridge. "What's the matter?" he asked. "Why didn't you chase those guys?"

Joe told him as he opened the trunk and pulled out the spare tire.

"Hey, a car's coming!" Frank said, running onto the bridge. He raised his hand and a speedy little sports car squealed to a stop.

"Give me a lift? We've got a flat."

"Hop in," said a middle-aged man.

Frank turned to his brother and Chet. "Meet

me in Centerville. I'm going to find out where
that car went!"

Frank stepped into the car, and the driver continued in the direction which the black sedan had
taken only a few minutes before. Without reveal-
ing the details, Frank told the driver the boys had
been robbed. Upon hearing this, the man speeded
up. When they came to the brow of a small hill,
Frank saw the sedan crossing a bridge about a mile
away.

"There they go!"

The excitement of the chase stimulated the
sports car driver. He went even faster. But they
could not overtake the sedan. At a crossroad,
Frank's keen eyes spotted the telltale marks of a
swerving car.

"They turned in here," he said.

The man braked, backed up, looked at the skid
marks, and agreed with Frank.

"But," he added, "I must keep on this road to
Hilton. Wish I could follow that car, but I have
an urgent appointment."

"Then let me out here," Frank said. "Many
thanks for the lift!"

The man sped off. Frank examined the marks of
the thieves' tires in the dirt road. After noting the
design of the treads for further identification, he
set off along the road at a trot. A half mile farther
on, he paused again at another crossroad, picking

out the tread along the right-hand fork, and hurried on.

After following the tire tracks about a mile, Frank stopped short. The lines suddenly left the road and slewed off into a thicket.

Entering the woods, he proceeded with caution, to avoid any possible danger of ambush. The tracks led into a thick copse, interspersed with scrubby trees. Except for a few birds and a scampering squirrel, there was not a sound. Ahead, under a low-hanging tree, Frank found the parked sedan. It was deserted.

He scraped away the mud on the license plate and jotted down the number, then studied the footprints near the sedan. They were hard to follow, for the thieves seemed to have separated at this point. Frank chose to follow the deepest prints, which presently led back to the side of the road. From here they ran straight, skirting the old battlefield of Rocky Run. Then, strangely, they were gone completely.

As Frank stood debating what to do next, he realized that the museum was located directly to the right. Had the thieves gone there to investigate?

"I'll see what's going on, anyway," Frank thought. "That professor and the guard sure are phonies."

As he walked along, he mulled over the events of the past few hours. Frank was convinced there might be a tie-in between the man who had grabbed the bandoleer and the professor. This time he would spy on the place, and perhaps learn something important.

Frank jumped a ditch beside the road and hid behind a tree. After glancing around cautiously and seeing nobody, he pressed his way along a field fence toward the old building.

No one was in sight. The windows were closed and locked, as well as the cellar door. Deciding to risk a look inside the old headquarters, Frank went quietly around to the front door. It stood open, and the guard was not there. He listened— not a sound. He slipped inside.

From somewhere in the building came an indistinct but angry voice. "You fool . . . the secret . . . you bungle everything, Smiley!"

The voice was that of Junior, alias Jimmy of the shoot.

"I tell you it ain't safe to carry it!" Smiley cried out. "Nobody'd think of lookin' for it among the souvenirs," he declared.

Excitedly Frank darted around the room. He glanced at all the tables and looked under the large exhibits for the stolen bandoleer. Suddenly his eyes spotted something unusual in the display case where he had picked up the old canteen. A Confederate cap was tilted at a peculiar angle. Frank lifted it. Underneath lay the silver cap box!

Frank let out a low whistle as he grasped the box, then tiptoed toward the door.

Just before he reached the end of the room, a section of the floor in front of him raised up. Smiley popped out of a trap door!

Frank side-stepped him neatly, but the man spotted the cap box in the boy's hand.

"You're not getting away with that!" Smiley snarled, and lunged toward him.

Smiley was almost upon Frank. But with head down and arms in front of him, the boy hit the man with the force of a fullback plowing through the line. Smiley grunted, reeled, and fell.

Frank bolted through the door, ready for his next opponent. No one was in sight!

His long legs fairly flew down the road. He looked back and saw someone following, but maintained his pace. His pursuer was finally lost from sight.

Frank did not slacken his speed until he was half a mile away. Then he settled down to an easy lope, tightly clutching the cap box.

Presently he came to the highway leading into Centerville. Frank had not gone far when he heard the sound of a car. Apprehension gripped him. Had the thieves caught up with him?

Frank hid behind a hedge and waited, his heart pounding like a riveting machine. As the car approached, he gave a whoop of joy. It was the Hardys' convertible!

"Hi there!" he called out, stepping into the road.

Joe jammed on the brakes and Frank jumped in.

"I've got it!" he panted, showing his prize. "Get to the general as fast as you can!"

"Great work!" Joe cried, and sent the car speeding down the road.

As they drove, Frank told his brother and Chet how he had trailed the thieves and seized the precious relic.

"There's no doubt now that Junior and Smiley —that's the guard's name—are mixed up in this thing. Probably the professor is in with them, too," he said. "And we know Dr. Bush is an enemy."

The boys reached the house and ran in with the bandoleer's ammunition box. The general was both elated and astonished at their find.

When the officer heard the story, he lost no time informing the chief of police of the strange doings at the old museum and reporting the license number of the black sedan. "I think these men might belong to a gang headed by a Dr. Bush," General Smith reported.

Chet felt relieved and hoped the troublemakers would be arrested or leave when they saw the police checking on them. But Frank and Joe were of a different opinion.

"The missing gold is a big prize," Frank

pointed out. "If that's what they're after, they won't be frightened into running away."

"They'll probably go into hiding at some new place around Centerville," Joe reasoned.

"I wasn't much of a detective," General Smith remarked about his own investigation of Professor Randolph. "The museum seemed to be running the same as ever when I visited it. The old Negro was there and everything was peaceful. I didn't pick up a single clue."

Joe smiled ruefully. "Smiley wasn't on guard because he and Junior were probably the two we chased after they attacked Chet and took the bandoleer."

Frank went to the kitchen and asked Claude for silver polish and a cloth. The others followed and watched as he went to work on the ammunition box. In a few minutes the old souvenir, blackened by its long concealment in the bridge abutment, shone brightly.

"Why'd you do that?" Chet asked.

"So we can examine it better," Frank said. "Joe, will you get our magnifying glass?"

His brother went to the trunk of the car and returned with a special kit the Hardys always carried. From it he took a powerful magnifier. Frank held the ammunition box under a bright light and went over it in minute detail.

"I think I see where you open this," he stated at last.

"Where?" Chet questioned, looking over his shoulder.

"Right here in the corner." Frank pointed to a tiny circle cleverly worked into one edge of the box. "Now if the spring hasn't rusted, this ought to do it!"

He snapped out the can-opener blade of his knife and carefully pressed the point against the circle. With a sharp click that startled the onlookers, the top of the box sprang open.

"Bravo!" the general shouted.

Joe emitted a low whistle. "No wonder those crooks couldn't open it."

Frank pried a piece of folded parchment from the bottom of the box. The paper was in perfect condition despite the many years it had lain secreted. Frank handed it to General Smith.

"Just think," Joe said, "the last man to see this was your great-grandfather!"

The general did not reply. The boys were silent as they observed the solemn expression on his handsome, tanned face. Then he spoke.

"This is strange, very strange indeed. I suddenly had the feeling that I was standing in my great-grandfather's place, there in the old headquarters, when he put this paper into the ammunition box and made ready for battle."

Chet cleared his throat and fidgeted. He wanted to know what was on the paper.

"This is a great moment for me," the man went on. "I wonder what the message says."

The boys turned their eyes from the officer to a table on which he spread the paper.

"Look at that!" Joe exclaimed. "It's in code!"

CHAPTER XIII

Digging for Gold

SCRAWLED on the parchment were four sets of numbers, written in a row: 42236, 12223, 223, 222123.

Across the face of the message, written diagonally, were the large letters, C S A. As if that were not cryptic enough, two odd designs decorated the bottom of the page at either side. On the left were three muskets, stacked together like a sheaf of wheat. On the right was a strange-looking tree, at the base of which rested a round object.

"What a puzzler!" Chet cried. "It'll take all year to figure this out."

Frank thrust his fingers back through his dark hair. Joe knew his brother was concocting a plan.

"I'd suggest," Frank said, "that we all sit down separately and work on this. When we have some ideas, we'll get together."

"Very good," the general declared. "Let's make

four rough sketches so we can each work on one."

When this was done, the four sat in deep thought, each pondering over the secret message. The room was so quiet that the ticking of the clock sounded like a noisy metronome.

Suddenly Chet chuckled and burst out, "I've got it!"

"Let's hear it," Joe urged, grinning. "Probably another one of your brainstorms."

"It's this way," Chet began, winking at the officer. "The C S A stands for 'Can't Stand the Army.' The guns stacked up means they're going to stop fighting and sit down under that tree and eat breakfast. That big round thing's an egg."

The general and the Hardys burst into laughter.

"I knew plenty of privates who couldn't stand the army," General Smith said with a smile.

Then Joe asked, "What about the numbers?"

With a wave of his hand, Chet replied, "That's just to confuse us!"

When they had composed themselves, Frank said:

"Chet, I can't agree with all of your deductions, but the one about the tree—maybe you've got something there!"

"Right," Joe added. "The tree probably is a landmark for something."

Some time later a sudden smile crossed Frank's face. He reached for a pencil, and began to write down figures on a piece of scratch paper. He had barely finished working out a series of letters and numbers when he shouted:

"This is it!"

With the others crowding around, Frank showed what he had done with the coded message.

"I took the C S A to mean Confederate States America," he announced.

"I figured that far, too," General Smith remarked.

"Where does that get you?" Chet asked skeptically.

Frank followed his procedure with the point of his pencil. He pointed to the four sets of numbers: 42236, 12223, 223, and 222123.

"The first figure, four, stands for the fourth letter in Confederate States America," Frank explained, "That's F. The twenty-second letter is I, the third letter is N, and the sixth is D."

"That spells 'Find,' " Joe said eagerly.

"The rest is easy," Frank continued.

Frank reeled off the other numbers in the sequence; some, one digit at a time, others in pairs. Spelling out the letters as he went, and with the eyes of his onlookers widening with amazement, the boy read the message:

Find coin in iron.

"That's a grand piece of code breaking!" General Smith complimented. "Army Intelligence could use you!"

"But we have to fathom these other symbols, too," Frank reminded the others. "What do you make of the muskets, the tree, and that round thing?"

"My guess would be," his brother replied, "that those symbols tell us where the iron is."

"Near some old Civil War muskets," Chet suggested.

"Or under a tree," General Smith said. Then he added with a puzzled expression, "That's a queer-looking tree. Don't believe I ever saw one like it."

"I still think that round thing's an egg!" Chet persisted.

"Looks to me," Joe observed, "as if we're still behind the eight ball so far as finding the treasure is concerned. 'Find coin in iron' can mean a dozen different things."

"That's right," Frank agreed. "It might mean the money is buried in an iron box, or hidden in an iron mine, or in an old forge."

"It might be in an old blacksmith shop," Joe suggested. "They had one on the plantation, didn't they, General Smith?"

"Yes," the officer replied. "Every big plantation had a blacksmith shop. Wait—I have a map here of the old Smith place."

He pulled it from a desk drawer, and the boys eagerly scanned it. The map was an antiquated form of blueprint, drawn on heavy linen paper and well preserved. The layout of the buildings was clearly delineated, with the tiny, handwritten word *blacksmith* barely discernible where the general's finger pointed.

The Hardys were eager to investigate the spot at once, even to work through the night, but the general would not hear of it.

"Morning will be time enough," he insisted. "Now that we know our enemies don't have the secret, there's no need for such speed. Furthermore, maybe the police will have rounded up the men by then and we won't have to worry about their spying on us."

The Hardys agreed with their host that the investigation could wait until the following day, but they expressed doubt that the gang would be caught easily.

Claude, hearing the story, declared he would stay up all night and guard the house against a visit by the thieves. It was finally decided that the boys would stay on watch until one o'clock, then the orderly would take over.

That evening at dinner the Hardys ran Chet a close race on second and third helpings of Claude's superb cured ham and pecan pie.

All was peaceful during the night, and early the next morning the boys and the general were ready to start for the old plantation.

Before leaving, General Smith called the police to inquire if any of the gang had been caught. He was told that the thickly wooded area was being combed and all highways were being watched but so far the culprits were still at large. The abandoned black sedan had been traced by its license and identified as the property of a man who lived in a town near Bayport.

"A beautiful day!" the general observed as they drove along. "But we'll have to be on the watch every moment."

"Not like the day when Beauregard Smith hid the fortune," Joe said, "with the distant thunder of artillery and the smell of powder in the air."

Frank stepped on the brake and turned the car off the highway into the rutted lane that led to the plantation. Presently he pulled up in front of the weed-grown foundation of the old mansion itself.

They strode through the high grass toward the spot the blueprint had indicated as the plantation's smithy.

"This is the place," the general confirmed. He paced off the distance from the site of the barn.

"Nothing here but a lot of rocks," Chet complained. "How are we going to find anything in this mess?"

"Put your camera down," Frank suggested. "It'll swing against one of those stones and get smashed."

"That means you want me to work," Chet said ruefully as he took the hint and removed the camera strap from around his neck.

Frank winked at his brother. "Full of deductions, isn't he?"

"I gather from the old blueprint that the walls of the shop were ten feet high," General Smith declared. "When the place was attacked, I suppose the walls fell in under a bombardment, so whatever was inside should be at the bottom of this rubble."

"Let's get at this pile," Joe said, pointing to a heap of crumbling masonry.

In order to avoid a surprise visit by their enemies, General Smith suggested they take turns standing guard. He took the first shift.

The three boys pulled and hauled, removing stone after stone as they delved deeper into the ruins of the old shop. The general walked around and around the spot, keeping an eye out for Bush, Randolph, Smiley, or Junior.

"Wow! This is hard work!" Chet exclaimed as perspiration ran down his forehead and off the end of his stubby nose. "It's going to take us years to find anything here," he moaned, straining at another stone.

Nevertheless, he stuck to the job and the four worked with silent intensity as the sun rose higher and higher. Finally the officer called a halt, and the group sat down to eat the lunch Claude had packed for them. After a rest period, during which Joe remained on guard, work started again.

"Here's a handle!" Frank said an hour later,

grasping a wooden pole that extended out of the ruins.

"That may be part of the forge!" Joe called excitedly.

Further digging disclosed the rest of the furnace. Somewhat later Joe came upon the anvil, which was so heavy it took the concerted efforts of the four to lift it.

"Do you suppose the gold's in this?" Chet asked eagerly.

"No," Frank replied. "This is a solid piece of iron."

As he spoke, Joe shouted, "Here's an old rifle!"

"Now we're getting somewhere!" Frank cried excitedly, recalling the stacked weapons on the coded message.

Feverishly the boys dug near the spot where the rusty old firearm had been exhumed.

At four o'clock Chet was ready to give up, when suddenly his hand struck something hard and smooth. He dug at it like a bulldog after a buried bone.

"I've found a box!" he shouted.

CHAPTER XIV

A Bombardment

JOE and Frank rushed to Chet's side. The three lifted the heavy iron box out of the rubble.

"I'll help you open it," General Smith offered, as excited as the boys in anticipation of discovering the Civil War gold.

The officer picked up a flat stone, and with a mighty blow, knocked off one of the rusty hinges. Chet pulled up the lid as the others looked on, holding their breath in anticipation.

Inside the box were a dozen horseshoes!

"Gosh!" Chet cried, a pout of disappointment thrusting his lower lip forward. "Why would anybody put horseshoes in a strongbox?"

"Just for luck." Joe grinned.

"Maybe they were used as weights," Frank suggested hopefully. "Let's see if there's anything underneath them."

Quickly lifting the horseshoes from the box, he

found a piece of rawhide. Beneath it, in the bottom of the box, lay a sheaf of papers.

"This was probably the box where the blacksmith kept his records," the general said as he read through the papers.

There were bills for barrels of nails, bars of iron, and other material used in the old shop. The last piece of paper read:

> *From Enfield Arms Co., Berkley, Eng.*
> *30 rifles*
> *100 cannon balls*
> *Taken to arsenal.*

Seeing the word "arsenal," General Smith's countenance took on a look of renewed interest.

"So old Beauregard had his own personal arsenal! That's news to me."

"There wasn't one on the blueprint," Joe commented.

"It must have been one of the plantation's secrets," Frank said.

"I can understand why," General Smith reasoned. "Whoever controlled the arsenal controlled the plantation!"

"I think this is a hot clue," Frank spoke up. "The round designs on the message may have represented cannon balls. Those, and the stacked rifles, may have referred to the arsenal! If we could find it, we might discover the gold, or at least directions to it."

"Where could the arsenal be?" Joe asked, puzzled.

"Probably a long distance from the plantation buildings," the general reasoned, "and underground. In the first place, it would be dangerous to store explosives near the main buildings, and secondly, arms and ammunition would probably be in a secret spot. I'd suggest we go home and study the blueprint for clues. Also," he added with a look at Chet, "Claude wouldn't want us to be late for dinner!"

"General Smith," Chet said, beaming, "I'd like to be in your army!" The boy picked up his camera. "But before we go, I want somebody to take a photo of me holding this clue."

Chet posed by the box he had unearthed while Joe held the camera.

"This is the last one on the film," Joe observed. "You'd better not move."

But just as he snapped the picture, Chet sneezed. General Smith shook his head as he smilingly led the group to the car.

As they started off, Chet asked the officer where he could have his prints made up.

"The general store in Centerville does its own developing. If we drop them off now, you could probably pick them up tonight."

"That's great. I'll get some more film too," Chet said.

When they arrived home, Frank noticed a letter lying on the hall table. It was addressed to the Hardys. He opened it, frowned, and read aloud:

" *'Hardy Boys,*
Clear out and go back to Bayport if you want
to stay healthy. Kids who don't mind their
own business end up in the graveyard.' "

The message was unsigned.

"Good night!" Joe exploded.

"S-somebody doesn't like you," Chet stammered.

"What's the postmark?" General Smith asked, taking the envelope. "Centerville, eh?"

"Which means," Frank reasoned, "that Bush or his men haven't left town. Let's call the police and see if they've arrested anyone."

The chief informed the general, who telephoned, that no one had returned to the museum nor had anyone fitting the description of Randolph, Smiley, or Junior been picked up.

"So they're still at large," General Smith said reflectively as he reported to the boys. "Now that this note has come—"

"We'll have to get Bush before he gets us!" Joe burst out.

"But we've got to act fast," Frank added.

"I admire your spirit." General Smith smiled. "Your plan of taking the offensive is in the best military tradition. An offense is sometimes the best defense. But we'll have to be doubly alert."

"I wish we knew what this Dr. Bush looks like," Frank mused. "But all we know is that he has long legs and carries a black bag."

"And probably has a number of aliases," Joe added.

"I'd like to get a picture of the other half of him," Chet remarked. "Which reminds me. I'll run into town after dinner and see if my prints are done."

Later, leaving the Hardys and the general mulling over their plan of attack, Chet took the convertible and drove to Centerville. He parked in front of the town's general store and went inside. Finding his prints ready, Chet paid the bill. While waiting for the change, he glanced around the store.

Everything from jellybeans to lawn chairs cluttered the establishment. Finally Chet's eyes fell on a string of tiny red balls hanging from a wooden rack.

"What are they?" he asked the clerk.

"Atom crackers."

"Atom crackers? Do you eat 'em?"

"I should say not," replied the small man dryly. "If you ate those, they'd blow you inside out!"

"I get it," Chet said, laughing. "They're like firecrackers."

"Only quite a bit louder," replied the man. "Want some? Fourth of July'll be here soon."

Chet beamed as he thought of scaring the Hardys with the powerful little charges.

"I'll take a dozen."

The man put twelve of the little red balls in a bag and handed it to Chet. As the boy went out the door, the shopkeeper warned him to be careful with them and get away quickly once he had lighted the fuse.

Intrigued by the thought of setting off a firecracker, Chet reached into the bag and pulled one out as soon as he reached the sidewalk. He had not noticed that directly across the street was the Centerville Police Station.

Grinning, Chet put the atom cracker on the sidewalk and lit the fuse. At the same time, he hopped back and lifted his hands to his ears. But as he did, the paper bag slipped from his fingers and landed directly on top of the sputtering fuse!

In an instant, the Centerville square shook with deafening explosions like a town under siege. Chet shuddered at every blast, hoping no more would go off, but the whole dozen sent their rapid-fire reverberations echoing and re-echoing through the little town.

"Oh! Oh no!" Chet moaned, seeing people pop their heads out of doors and windows.

The exclamation was hardly off his lips when three policemen came storming from the station house. Two other officers followed, which gave

Chet shuddered at every blast

the boy the feeling that he was being ushered to his doom.

"But I d-didn't mean to do anything," he said with outstretched hands.

"Tell that to the chief."

Chet was marched into the police station and led across the room to a desk perched on a dais.

"This boy is responsible for that bombardment!" one policeman bellowed.

The chief, a stout man with three distinct chins, leaned forward and looked over his horn-rimmed glasses at the trembling boy.

"This is a clear case of disturbing the peace! I'm going to throw you in jail!" he shouted angrily.

CHAPTER XV

A Shot in the Dark

"Don't put me in jail!" Chet pleaded. He visualized himself spending the summer behind bars. "Please, Chief, if I go to jail, I won't be able to get pictures of the criminals."

The man raised his eyebrows and the police officers exchanged questioning glances.

The chief leaned far over his desk and shook a finger at Chet. "If there are any pictures of criminals to be taken, you'd better leave it to the police!" he stormed.

"I take it you're one of General Smith's guests," he added less sternly.

"Yes, sir," Chet answered.

"Well, I'm going to let you go this time. But only on one condition—no more atom crackers before the Fourth of July!"

"Yes, sir!" The boy sighed in relief.

As Chet was leaving, the chief called to him. "Will you be seeing General Smith tonight?"

"Yes, sir."

"Tell him that a woman called here a little while ago and warned us to pick up Dr. Bush if he came around. She wouldn't give us her name."

Chet told the chief that a similar request had come to the Hardys in Bayport.

"We're searching for Randolph and those other two," the chief said. "You boys keep your eyes open too."

"We sure will," Chet promised as he left.

On the sidewalk he came face to face with the Hardys, who were out of breath from running.

"You all right, Chet?" Frank panted. "We heard a bombardment. What happened? Who started it?"

"I did!"

"What?"

"I learned you shouldn't shoot off atom crackers here before the Fourth of July."

With much laughter, the Hardys finally got Chet's story straight. He also told them about the woman's phone call. There was no doubt in anyone's mind that Bush was in the vicinity. But who, Frank and Joe wondered, was the mysterious woman? The boys decided to discuss the matter at the house.

"I got my pictures," Chet beamed.

"Let's see 'em," Frank said.

Chet pulled the packet from his pocket, and held the photos under a street light. Of all the snaps the boy had taken, only a few had proved clear enough to print. One showed the old museum; another the ruins of the plantation; and a third, a hawk which Chet had snapped in mid-air.

"What's this funny-looking thing?" Joe asked, holding up another print.

"Gee, I don't know," Chet scratched his head.

"It's upside down," Frank remarked.

"Now I see it!" Chet bubbled. "I must have taken this when I backed into the wellhole. Look! There's the guy who was spying on me!" He pointed to a thick mass of foliage.

"You're right," Frank agreed. "There are a man's back and shoulders, and part of his legs."

"Another half-man," Chet moaned.

"Say!" Joe's eyes lit up. "I wonder if this is the same man you got a picture of in Bayport."

"We'll soon find out," Chet said, pulling the duplicate of the stolen print from his pocket.

"The legs seem to match," Joe observed. "At least now we know that Bush has not only long legs but high, square shoulders."

"If I'd only gotten his face!" Chet groaned.

"Don't worry," Frank offered encouragingly. "We have two strikes on Bush now. Next time you'll get his face."

As Chet put all his photographs into the envelope, Joe went across the street to buy some atom crackers. He returned in a few minutes with a bagful.

"Let me see 'em," Chet begged.

"No sirree," Joe insisted, shoving the bag into his pocket. "These are for the Fourth."

Upon reaching the house, Chet related his experience in town to the general. The officer laughed heartily at the story of the atom crackers, but frowned upon hearing of the woman's phone call.

"With Bush and his gang still around, we're going to have to be prepared for anything."

Later that night, the boys decided to take a drive around the Centerville area. The stars were clear and the air felt refreshingly cool as they leisurely toured the countryside in the open convertible.

On the way home, Frank decided to go past the old Beauregard Smith plantation. Soon they were approaching the overgrown lane which led into the property.

"Well, tonight I can get a good, solid sleep." Chet yawned. "No more sleuthing until tomorrow."

"Don't be too sure," Frank said, slowing down. "I just saw a light flash in there! Let's see what's going on."

As he pulled to the side of the road, Chet

grunted and announced he would guard the car while the Hardys went to investigate.

"Sure! Fall asleep and be kidnapped," Joe teased. "You'd better come along."

"But I'm tired, fellows."

Chet reluctantly agreed and brought up the rear as the boys, unlighted flashlights in hand, walked silently and cautiously toward the spot where Frank had seen a light.

The clear, star-studded sky made it easy for them to find their way. When they reached the front of the mansion's ruins, Chet flopped down on a granite stepping-stone. He yawned, and his head flopped down onto his ample chest.

No light was visible, but there were muffled sounds.

"Sombody's digging!" Joe whispered.

"For the lost gold, I'll bet." Chet came to life. "Let's rush 'em!"

"We'd better wait here awhile," Frank advised. "Nobody can see us, and we may be able to pick up some useful information."

The boys strained their ears. A thud sounded emptily in the distance. Then another.

Suddenly Chet sneezed. In the stillness, the sound seemed magnified a hundred times. The thuds stopped.

"Quick! Move to another place!" Frank ordered. "They've spotted us!"

As he grabbed Chet by the arm and pulled him roughly from his perch on the stepping-stone, a flash winked in the distance and the sound of a rifle shot shattered the stillness.

"I'm hit!" Chet cried out, falling to the ground.

"Where?"

"In the leg." Chet writhed in pain.

Apprehension gripped the Hardys. Had their friend been badly wounded? It would take both to carry him to their car. Meanwhile, what about the diggers?

"First things first," Frank said, gritting his teeth.

Forgetting all other problems, the brothers hauled Chet to his feet and put an arm over each of their shoulders. At a safe distance from the rifleman, they laid him on the ground.

"Hurry. Get me to a doctor," Chet moaned.

Frank, using his body to shield the beam of his flashlight, bent low to examine the wound.

Blood oozed from above the right knee, but there was only a long, deep scratch on Chet's leg.

"You weren't shot, Chet." Frank tried to conceal his grin. "You've scratched your leg on the stepping-stone. Hold on—I'll bandage it."

"I'm not shot?" Chet sat up in surprise.

"Are you disappointed?" Joe asked.

"Guess not," Chet replied as Frank bound the wound with a clean handkerchief. He added,

"Thanks, fellows. Didn't mean to scare you like that."

"Forget it," Frank said. He turned to his brother. "Joe, put an ear to the ground."

The blond boy obeyed. Receding footsteps told him there were at least two enemies. Then dull thuds made it evident they had gone back to their work.

"Come on! Let's find that guy who shot at us!"

"Right! Chet, you stay here till we get back."

"But they're armed!" Chet argued. "You haven't got a chance against them!"

"We'll be careful," Frank promised. "We have to find out who they are and what they're up to."

With that, the Hardys slipped into the darkness, circling toward the spot from which the rifle flash had come.

CHAPTER XVI

An Old Safe

"LISTEN!"

Frank grabbed Joe's arm, and the boys stood stock-still. Work was going on in a pit among the ruins of the plantation's former study.

"Sure I scared 'em off," a man said braggingly. "Pretty brave till they heard my gun."

"Good thing we got the stones blasted out before they came," another said.

"I just hit something, Hank! Gimme your strong light."

Junior! And another of the boys' kidnappers!

In a moment a glow sprang up not more than twenty feet from the Hardys. Frank and Joe crouched low to avoid detection, all the while observing the bizarre scene before them. The two men, their backs toward the boys, were stooping down in a hole dug along an inside cellar wall of the house.

"It's a safe, Hank!" Junior said excitedly.

"Jumping jiminy!" Joe whispered to his brother. "If they've found the gold, we've got to act fast!"

The boys backed away and held a hurried consultation. It was decided that they had better try to stop the criminals from opening the safe rather than go for the police.

"But how?" Frank pondered.

"I've got it!" Joe said softly. "The atom crackers!"

Frank immediately grasped his brother's idea. "We'll scare them off! Careful, Joe. If they see the light of the match, we're sunk."

The younger boy pulled the bag of atom crackers from his pocket and crouched at the very base of the wall so that the light of his match could not be seen by the men.

When the fuse of the little red ball sputtered, Joe hurled it toward the edge of the woods about fifty feet from where Junior and his companion were standing.

One second, two seconds, then—*wham!*

The diggers jumped and cursed, as Joe lit the second cracker.

"Sh-shoot back at 'em, Junior!"

Joe lobbed the cracker. Junior reached for his rifle. As he did, a second explosion burst from the opposite direction, and then a third from still another direction.

"We're surrounded!" he cried out. "We'd better scram."

As if to help the men on their way, a fourth atom cracker burst behind them, filling the night with a thousand reverberations. The boys thought of following to nab at least one of them, but both started shooting over their shoulders as they fled.

Frank and Joe stopped running. Regretfully, they watched the erratic course of the men's firing as the two fled to the road, scrambled into an automobile, and roared off.

"Let's get our car!" Joe urged.

Frank reminded his brother of the distance to their car and the fact that Chet was alone, his leg injured.

"I'd say we ought to have a look at that safe before Junior and Hank decide to return with reinforcements."

"You're right," Joe agreed.

The Hardys went back to Chet, who was in a near-panic because of the shooting. Relieved to see his friends safe, the boy declared he could limp with little pain and insisted upon going to the pit and watching.

"This sure is an old safe," Frank declared as he climbed down into the hole and examined the large, rusted object with its old-fashioned dial.

Excitedly the boys looked around for tools the diggers might have left, so they could open the safe. They found nothing but two spades, which were of no help.

"Tell you what," Chet spoke up. "You fellows stay here. I'll go tell General Smith what happened. He'll probably want to come out here, and we can bring tools."

"Good idea," Frank said. "You stay home and take care of that wound."

Chet's leg was swelling and had begun to ache. When he reached the car, he gave a couple of blasts on the horn to let the Hardys know he had reached it safely, then drove off.

Frank and Joe figured that the general would arrive by midnight, but two hours went by and he did not come. Had Chet been waylaid? the brothers wondered.

Finally the boys could no longer stand the suspense of waiting, and started for the road. They had just made the turn toward Centerville when a car came along.

Ducking behind some bushes, they let it go past without hailing the driver. There must be no more mishaps tonight!

"It's our car," Frank whispered. "Look, it's turning into the lane!"

The Hardys followed on a run. The condition of the overgrown road was so bad that the car had to crawl along, with the result that the boys easily caught up to it. General Smith was at the wheel. When he stopped, Frank opened the door.

"We were worried about you, sir," he said. "Is Chet all right?"

"Yes, and being attended to by Claude at home. But he arrived with an empty gas tank. What a time I had getting some at this hour of the night! Well, let's get to work. I understand we're on the brink of finding the long-lost gold!"

In the back of the car were a crowbar, sledge hammer, file, a blowtorch, and some rope which General Smith had borrowed from the garageman who had sold him the gasoline. The boys lugged the equipment to the pit, and pointed out the safe, which had been craftily concealed in a wall.

"It's not going to be easy to open this," the officer said as he stood in front of it. "And the noise may attract attention."

The general ordered Frank to stand guard, while he and Joe worked. Fifteen minutes later the blowtorch had failed to make a hole, but Frank thought they might crack through the hot iron. Joe replaced him as guard.

"Hold this chisel at the edge of the dial, General Smith, while I swing the sledge hammer," Frank requested.

The officer held the chisel unflinchingly while Frank, his sure eye guiding the heavy tool, hit one crashing blow after another. The steel dial gave way grudgingly, but finally, with a mighty stroke, Frank knocked it off the rusty safe.

With a little prying, the bolt came loose and Frank pulled on the door. It creaked open. He half expected a cascade of gold to tumble into his hands, but instead only a bundle of old papers greeted his eyes!

"Here's a book," he said, reaching farther back into the safe. Frank opened it and flipped the pages as General Smith trained his flashlight on the discovery.

"A diary!" Frank exclaimed. Hastily he read the entries in the old book, apparently written by Beauregard Smith himself. Recorded were the daily happenings on the plantation. With the mentioning of the advance of the enemy army, the remarks became terse. Some days' events were listed in only a sentence or two. Finally the last entry in the old diary said simply:

Despairing, have taken cannon balls to tunnel. Sent message to General Smith.

Frank whistled. "What a clue! Joe, come here!" he cried out.

"First an arsenal. Now a tunnel," General Smith said. "This is getting more baffling as we go along."

"The arsenal might *be* a tunnel," Joe said, after reading the notation.

"I have an idea," Frank declared, "that the gold and a lot of old cannon balls are lying side by side in some secret tunnel. Tomorrow we'll have to start some real digging."

"The sooner the better!" Joe exclaimed.

"I'll hire a couple of laborers to help us," General Smith offered, "and we'll dig this place up till we find that tunnel!"

The eastern sky was faintly pink as the group gathered up the papers and set off for the car. Back home they bathed, ate, and caught a few hours' sleep. Then the general made some telephone calls to arrange for two workmen in Centerville to help with the digging on the plantation.

Chet, who was the last one awake, was agog over the news. Though his leg was stiff and sore, he insisted upon going with the group to hunt for the tunnel.

Directly after breakfast, they set out for town to pick up the two workmen. On the way, the Hardys discussed with General Smith where the tunnel might be.

"It's hard to say," the officer said. "I would imagine it led from the cellar of the mansion to one of the other buildings. Or it might have been an underground entrance for slaves coming to the house."

A few minutes later, having picked up the laborers, they drove to the old plantation.

"I want you to dig in the ruins of this mansion," the general told the men. "We think there may be an old tunnel here somewhere."

The laborers plied picks and shovels, and the

boys pitched in to aid in the arduous task. Together they dug in the hot sun until late in the
morning when Joe's pick struck a layer of bricks.

"Hand me a crowbar!" he called up to Chet,
who was sitting on a pile of stones watching the
work.

His friend let down the long bar. Joe pried at
the bricks by his feet. Suddenly they caved in and
the crowbar plopped into a deep hole.

"I've hit a tunnel!" Joe cried.

CHAPTER XVII

A Fresh Perspective

THE opening Joe had made in the earth was large enough for him to slip through. He beamed his flashlight below. There definitely was an underground passageway!

"Lower me down here, Frank," he called excitedly.

Frank and Joe interlocked their wrists, the older boy easing his brother down into the black hole.

"Okay," Joe called hollowly in the vault below. "I've hit bottom. It's solid."

"What do you see?"

Joe flashed a beam around the moss-covered walls of the tunnel.

"Nothing here," he shouted. "But I'll find out where it goes."

"Wait for me," Frank urged.

In a moment he, too, was in the tunnel. The

boys turned left and walked gingerly in the bricked passageway toward what once apparently had been the opening into the cellar of the mansion. The entrance was sealed up by a heap of stones which had fallen down from the old foundation.

"This is as far as we go in this direction," Joe said. "Let's find the exit."

Picking their way along the dark tunnel, the boys walked nearly two hundred feet. There was no sign of gold or of any cannon balls. Presently the passageway started uphill.

"Here's a dead end," Frank concluded as they came to a halt before a mound of earth.

"But it must lead somewhere," Joe insisted. "I'm going to give it a kick." He sent his foot thudding into the soft dirt. "Look! I see daylight!"

Joe's kick had opened a slight fissure in the earthwork at the end of the tunnel.

He stood back a few feet, then ran forward, twisting so that his shoulder hit the dirt wall with a solid impact. The end of the tunnel gave way and Joe went sprawling.

Frank quickly followed. When the boys' eyes became accustomed to the sunlight, they realized they were at the foot of a small terrace behind the ruins of the plantation house.

"This knoll probably was built just to conceal the opening to that tunnel," Frank remarked.

"And it's concealing something else," Joe whispered excitedly. "Look!"

Frank followed his brother's gaze to a figure crouched behind a tree, apparently observing every move of the two diggers, Chet, and the general. He was thin, and had a stubbly gray beard.

Joe started toward the man, but in his haste stepped on a twig, which snapped with the sound of a revolver shot. The watcher looked around. When he saw Frank and Joe coming toward him, the man took to his heels.

Hearing the sound of crashing brush, the others at the ruins turned in surprise to see the Hardys racing after a stranger.

"How the dickens did they get out of that tunnel?" Chet spluttered.

As the laborers watched open-mouthed, Frank and Joe sped after the fugitive, who seemed to be following a familiar route. Though a swift runner, he was no match for the Hardys. In a few minutes they overtook him.

"Lemme go!" he cried loudly as the boys held on to him. "I ain't done nothin'!"

The boys recognized the voice as that of Hank, the man who had been with Junior when they discovered the safe.

"Why were you spying on us?" Frank demanded.

"None o' your business what I do for the pro—"

The man caught himself and refused to say another word.

"Pro?" Frank thought. On a hunch, he said, "Better talk, Hank! We know you're working for Professor Randolph."

Frank's deduction evidently had been correct. A wild look came into their prisoner's eyes. He made a desperate effort to escape, but the Hardys tightened their grip and escorted the man back to the ruins.

General Smith met the trio a distance away from the laborers. "Brought in a prisoner, eh?"

Frank whispered to the officer, "I'm sure he's one of the gang. He was watching us work."

The general tried to make the man talk, but it was useless. He decided to turn the fellow over to the police at once. Since the Hardys wanted to investigate the tunnel farther, they remained at the spot.

After the prisoner's hands and legs had been firmly tied, Chet, as custodian, went along with the general to Centerville.

Frank and Joe looked carefully at every brick in the old tunnel but found no clue to the treasure.

"I don't think this is the tunnel old Beauregard Smith meant," Joe said at last.

While the boys waited for General Smith to return, they discussed the mystery from every angle. Perhaps now they would get a break, if the prisoner would tell all he knew. They were still discussing the capture when the general returned alone, Chet having remained at the police station to provide the chief with full information.

"But even if he doesn't talk, we know he's one of the Bush gang," Joe declared.

"I don't like Bush's silence," Frank spoke up. "It's kind of ominous. I think we ought to checkmate him."

"Good idea," the general agreed. "But how?"

Frank mulled over the problem.

"The man we captured seemed to be heading for a definite destination. Perhaps Bush and his gang have a hideout right under our noses."

"It would be mighty hard to ferret them out," the officer said. "They're probably in a secluded place where they'd have the draw on us. If it's in the timberland, it would take an army to beat the bush."

"Unless we got high enough to look down on them," Frank suggested.

"A plane!" Joe was excited as he informed the general that both he and Frank were experienced pilots.

"But the noise would give you away before you reached them," the officer objected.

"There's nothing to make them suspect we'd be flying," Frank declared.

"I've noticed several private planes around here

in the past week. Is there an airport nearby, General Smith?"

"Yes, a big one about twenty miles from Rocky Run. Why don't you do it this afternoon? I think there's been enough gold hunting for one day."

When they arrived home, Chet handed the Hardys a telegram. It said:

GOOD CLUE. JUNIOR OLDER. WEST TRAILS SLIPPERY. DOWN SOON. DAD.

Chet grinned. "Gee, that sounds funny. I suppose it's in code."

Neither he nor the general could make out the message, so Frank interpreted. "Junior is older than he appears and a slippery customer, probably from out West."

"Wow!" Chet cried. "No wonder he's handy with a gun!"

General Smith looked very serious. "You boys have done mighty well on this case, and have one prisoner. Don't you want to call it quits? With the material you've already gathered, your dad should solve this mystery in short order."

Joe frowned. "That's just it, sir. *We* want to solve it before he gets here."

"Well, I'm all for you," the officer said happily. "You surely have opened my eyes. Didn't know the younger generation had so much detective ability. We'll get that plane this afternoon. Call up and make arrangements, Frank."

The boy contacted the airport and talked with a young pilot who operated a plane-leasing service. He readily agreed to rent the Hardys a small plane.

At four o'clock Frank, Joe, and Chet arrived at the airport. By arrangement, General Smith was to post himself at the old plantation. If the boys found the location of Bush's hideout, they were to fly over the plantation and drop a message to the officer. He, in turn, was to get the local police to assist in the roundup of the criminals.

On the way to the airport building, Chet chattered eagerly. "Just the kind of day for pictures. Maybe I can take some good ones from the plane and sell them to the local newspaper."

A young man came out the door of a hangar as Frank parked. He smiled at the boys, and introduced himself as Tom Crandall.

Frank briefly explained his mission, saying they were going to look for a group of men believed to be in the woods near the old plantation.

"You can go up right away. There's your baby. I checked her out myself." Crandall indicated a sleek little silver four-seater.

The boys strode out to the runway apron and climbed aboard. Frank started the engine, the propeller raced to life, and the small craft shuddered with power.

"Okay, here we go!" Frank shouted as he taxied

to take-off position. In a few minutes the plane rose into the air.

Joe sat in the seat next to his brother, with Chet directly behind. As the craft glided over the tree-tops, Chet watched as Frank manipulated the controls.

"Gee I'd sure like to learn to fly these things," the boy mused.

"Nothing's stopping you!" Joe grinned, turning to wink at Frank.

"We'll crisscross the area," Frank said. "Sing out when you spot the Smith place."

"Boy, this is the life!" Chet beamed as he leaned toward a window to take photographs.

It did not take the craft long to reach the old plantation. Peering out, the boys saw General Smith far below, waving up to them.

"Here's the place," Frank said, taking in the area with a sweep of his hand. "I'll go a mile or so north, then back again. Keep a sharp lookout when we get over the middle of the woods."

The boys' eyes were glued to the windows for a possible glimpse of anybody in the secluded area below. Chet fussed with his telephoto lens, then squinted down at the scene.

Suddenly Frank cried out, "Look! There's smoke over there!"

Far ahead, and apparently rising from a clearing, curled a lazy wisp of smoke.

"Somebody's down there, sure as shootin'," Joe stated. "We'll pass right over them."

Tense with excitement, the boys waited for the plane to reach the spot from which the smoke was rising.

"Can you bring her lower?" Joe asked.

Frank nodded, then manipulated the controls so that the plane nosed gently down. He leveled off again. The smoke was closer. Finally a clearing came into view.

Frank decided not to fly over it directly. Instead he made a wide circle, banking at an angle to give all of them a clear view of the place.

"Well, would you look at that!" Chet said, and adjusted his telephoto lens.

Three men were around a campfire, evidently preparing a meal. The figures were bending over, so that they could neither be seen directly by the boys nor could they see the occupants of the plane bearing down upon them.

The shutter of Chet's camera clicked and clicked again. Suddenly the men, apparently now suspicious of the low-flying plane, grabbed up something from the ground and dashed into the bushes. But not before Chet had snapped another picture!

"What now?" asked Joe.

"Back to the plantation," Frank said. "We'll drop a note to General Smith."

Frank eased the plane into a banking turn, ap-

Three men hovered around a campfire

plied full throttle, and climbed for altitude. But as he did, a man on the ground ran into the clearing.

Chet centered him in the view finder and exclaimed. "He's got a rifle. He's aiming at us!"

All three could see tiny puffs of smoke as the high-power weapon spoke and bullets struck home against the fuselage. Then a bullet thudded against the straining motor. Frank gave a groan of dismay as the engine began to cough!

CHAPTER XVIII

A Final Clue

"THE bullet's hit the fuel line!" Frank shouted to Joe and Chet.

Immediately he tried to coax the engine back to its normal, pulsating drone, but his feverish manipulation failed. The sputtering became continuous, and the craft began to lose altitude.

"We're going to crash!" Chet cried hysterically.

"Pull yourself together," Joe shouted. "Frank can handle a plane as well as if he'd been born at the controls."

The older Hardy grinned at his brother's high praise, even as he himself began to lose hope.

"We may be able to keep her up long enough to make it back to the airstrip," he yelled encouragingly.

Yet as he fought to maintain a safe altitude, Frank knew that at any moment the engine might give a final cough, and quit. And there was the further danger that leaking gas from the damaged fuel line might ignite and set the small plane aflame.

"I can see the airport ahead now!" Joe exclaimed excitedly. "You're doing fine, Frank. Keep up—"

The boy's remark was cut short as the engine gave a sudden shudder and the craft dropped sharply. Trees loomed only a few feet beneath the belly of the plane.

But now Frank was lined up with the runway.

"Hang on!" he bellowed. "I think we're going to make it—but it may be a rough landing!"

Chet sucked in his breath and shut his eyes as the wheels struck the concrete and bounced. The plane bounced twice more, then skidded to a final stop a few yards in front of its hangar.

Frank heaved a huge sigh of relief as Joe clapped him on the back.

"Great work!"

"Y-you mean we-we're s-safe?" Chet asked unbelievingly as the boys helped him from the craft.

"I've had close calls, but this was the closest," Frank admitted.

Just then Crandall ran from the hangar.

"I'm sorry your plane's damaged," Frank said, and he explained what had happened.

Crandall managed a half-smile. "The plane's covered by insurance," he said. "I'm just glad you're all safe!"

As the Hardys and Chet made their way to the office, Crandall asked if they had any idea who had fired upon them.

"We think the man responsible is a criminal who calls himself Dr. Bush," Joe answered. "He and his cohorts have been bothering us for some time."

"Well," Crandall said after a pause, "Bush is in real trouble now. He can't go around shooting at planes and expect to get away with it!"

After settling the bill for the plane's rental and thanking Crandall, the three boys went to the police station and reported the incident. The chief said he would relay the information to the county sheriff and a determined search would be made for the men involved.

Frank and Joe wanted to join the hunt, but when they telephoned their news to General Smith, he would not hear of it.

"You were up most of last night," he reminded them. "Come on back here and get some rest."

Claude was waiting for them with a sumptuous meal. It was not Chet alone who came back for third helpings of pompano and fried tomatoes. Frank and Joe's recent experience had given them ravenous appetites.

Chet had planned to take his roll of film to town for developing after dinner, but he fell asleep in an easy chair. General Smith and Joe discussed the mystery, while Frank for the hundredth time looked over the coded message found in the ammunition box. Finally he said:

"There's one symbol on this sheet we've never tried to decipher and it might be the connecting link."

"What's that?" Joe asked.

"The strange-looking tree. You said you never saw one like it, General Smith?"

"I can't recall ever having seen one."

Frank became silent again, but in a few minutes he remarked, "Do you suppose there are any old-timers in town who would have any information about the plantation before it was ruined?"

As the general pondered, Claude came to say good night. "I beg your pardon," he said, "but I couldn't help hearing your conversation. I believe Reverend Colts, the pastor of my church, could help you."

"That's fine. Thank you, Claude. We'll call on him in the morning," the general said.

The Hardys' first stop the following day, however, was the jail. There they were told that Hank still refused to talk. The boys also learned there was no news of Bush or the gang.

While Chet went to the general store with film to be developed, the Hardys and General Smith called at the home of Reverend Colts. A middle-aged man answered their knock. The general introduced himself and asked the pastor if he knew of anyone still living who had had any contact with the Smith plantation years ago.

"Yes, I do," the pastor replied. "Benjamin Berry. He lives in an old folks' home. I'm quite sure his grandfather worked for Mr. Beauregard Smith."

The boys and the general thanked the pastor and drove to the home, located a mile away. An attendant pointed out old Ben, who was rocking on the side porch of the red-brick building.

"How do you do, Ben?" said General Smith. Smiling, he told the man who he was. "Meet some friends."

The old man nodded. To their questions, he replied that his grandfather had served the Beauregard Smith family long after the emancipation. He was delighted to talk of the older days. After a few minutes General Smith steered the conversation around to the lost tunnel.

"Did you ever hear of an old arsenal on the plantation?" the general asked.

Ben shook his head.

"Ever see a tunnel, or any other hiding place?"

The old man took up a cane resting beside his chair and thoughtfully folded his bony hands over its head.

"I'm tryin' to think, General." He paused. "No. I don't remember any tunnel, but I know my grandpop was scared of the woods along the run."

"Why?" Joe was first with the question.

"He said he once saw Mr. Beauregard swallowed right up by the earth, probably because of some hole that nobody but Mr. Smith knew about."

"That may be just what we're looking for!" Joe burst out. "Where was the place, Ben?"

"I don't know exactly. Some place along Rocky Run."

"There's another question we'd like to ask you, Ben," Frank spoke up. The boy reached into his pocket and pulled out a drawing of the tree as it had appeared on the coded message. "Ever see a tree like this?"

Ben carefully adjusted a pair of gold-rimmed spectacles on the bridge of his nose. After studying the tree a moment, he smiled.

"Well I declare! I haven't seen a Franklin tree for many, many a year."

"A Franklin tree?"

"Mr. Smith planted a lot of them along the Rocky Run. They were his favorite trees. But most of them died right off, so I heard."

Ben believed the species had been found growing first in the Carolinas. Then it had almost died out until the middle of the nineteenth century, when it became quite popular and was named for Benjamin Franklin.

"Could you describe the tree?" Joe asked.

The old man thought a moment.

"As I remember, the trees stood fifteen, twenty feet high. They had leaves like those on magnolias, with fragrant white blossoms." He concluded, "The trees are still rare, because they're hard to grow. It's too bad. They smelled wonderful on summer afternoons."

Ben looked up. "I'm sorry I haven't been able to be of more help to you."

"But you have!" Joe said enthusiastically.

After thanking Ben for his information, the trio got into the car and returned to Centerville. Chet was waiting for them in front of the store.

"Let's get out to Rocky Run as soon as possible," Joe said eagerly.

"Not me," Chet spoke up. "I have a hunch that this time my pictures are going to solve the mystery. The man said he'd have 'em ready by twelve o'clock, so I'm hanging around here to wait."

General Smith and the Hardys were about to drive off when Claude came hurrying along the street, waving for the officer to wait.

"A long-distance call came in for you, sir," he reported. "Very poor connection, but the party said he would call again about twelve. It's very important, and he asked that you please be there."

Telling Frank and Joe he would see them later, the general followed Claude.

As the Hardy boys drove off, they wondered if

the call might have anything to do with their case. But the thought left their minds as they eagerly talked about the clue of the Franklin tree.

In the meantime, Chet, to while away the time, walked around the town, had an ice-cream soda, and bought some scenic cards of Centerville to send home. At a quarter to twelve his pictures were ready.

Chet pulled them from the envelope eagerly. One look and he gave a shout.

"Randolph! The black bag! I've got to get to General Smith fast!"

CHAPTER XIX

The Lost Tunnel

CHET left the storekeeper staring open-mouthed at his cryptic remarks. The stout boy had never moved faster than he did in the next few minutes. Bursting breathlessly into General Smith's home, he was met by the officer who was just turning away from the telephone.

"Chet, we must find Frank and Joe at once!"

"What's up?" Chet replied, stopping short with the photographs in his hand. The look of worry on the general's face alarmed him.

"Mr. Hardy has uncovered the identities of our enemies. I've just had a message from his home. He's flying down here."

"Bush and his men are bank robbers, wanted on the West Coast," he continued. "They're fully armed and deadly! If we don't get to Frank and Joe immediately, we may never see them alive again!"

Meanwhile, the Hardys had covered a lot of ground. After hiding the car in a grove of trees, they had started their search along the north bank of Rocky Run, the side nearest the plantation buildings.

"Suppose you look for signs of a tunnel along the shore, Joe," his brother suggested. "I'll keep my eyes open for Franklin trees or other clues a little distance from the water."

The boys started upstream, carrying a shovel and a spade. Every little crevice among the rocks, every depression in the ground was carefully probed. When an old stone fence indicated they had come to the end of the plantation, Frank and Joe switched places and started back to recheck before crossing the stream.

They continued the search, looking at every tree and every inch of ground until their backs ached. Finally Frank called a halt. He went to the brink of the stream, bent down, and splashed his face with the cool water. The refreshing pause sharpened his senses. Taking in a deep breath of woodland air, he remarked:

"Smell that sweet honeysuckle?"

"Honeysuckle?" Joe repeated. Suddenly his eyes lighted with excitement. "Frank! Maybe what we smell is from the blossoms of a Franklin tree!"

"Joe, you're a whiz. But I didn't see any Franklin trees on this side of—"

"Let's look on the other side of the stream," Joe interrupted excitedly.

Following the direction from which the sweet scent seemed to be coming, they crossed the rapidly swirling water and pressed several yards into the woods. Suddenly Frank spotted something.

"Follow me!" he cried, scrambling through the brush.

He and Joe reached a beautiful tree, whose fragrance scented the woodland. Although the branches seemed to be decaying in several places, its leaves were large, with beautiful white blossoms. There were no other trees around like it.

"Maybe this is it!" Joe cried.

"The only one left of Beauregard Smith's favorite trees," Frank murmured in awe.

"Come on!"

Starting at the base of the tree, the boys made ever-widening circles, probing every inch of ground as they went.

"Hey, look at this!" Frank said as he came upon a large mossy mound close to the stream. Opening his knife, the boy peeled off some of the thick green sod. Underneath a layer of earth he found a brick.

The boys began to dig away the sod furiously. A few minutes later they had uncovered a vaultlike enclosure. They loosened the bricks in the front one by one. Finally they had made an opening large enough to squeeze through. The daylight which penetrated the darkness below revealed old stone steps leading downward.

"The lost tunnel! The arsenal!" Joe exulted hoarsely.

Frank was just as excited as his brother, but he warned Joe:

"Keep it down! We don't want to attract any of Bush's men—yet."

Joe already was leaping down the steps, Frank close behind.

They found themselves in a musty cavern. Both boys whipped out their flashlights, then halted in amazement.

"Cannon balls!" Frank exclaimed. "Look! There must be a hundred of them."

The balls were piled in a huge pyramid in the middle of the dank cave.

"But I don't see any gold," Joe said in disappointment, straining his eyes to catch every detail of the place.

The gloomy tunnel was a natural rock cavern which apparently had been enlarged for use as a storehouse. The Hardys went to the end, about fifty feet ahead. The exit was solidly blocked with stones, bricks, and earth. There seemed no evidence of the Smith fortune or the bank's gold anywhere in the cavern.

"Unless . . ." Frank said. "Joe! I have it! You remember the message, 'Find coin in iron'?"

He dashed back toward the entrance. At the same moment the sunlight was cut off. There came the sound of men's voices. Chilling words were projected into the tunnel.

"You've had your last chance, Hardys! We warned your father! Smiley, light the fuse!"

CHAPTER XX

The Plantation's Secret

THE screeching of brakes sounded in front of General Smith's house as a taxi came to a sudden stop. Chet and the officer looked out the window in time to see Fenton Hardy step out, tell the driver to wait, and dash to the front door. Behind him hurried Sam Radley, his operative.

"Frank and Joe!" were the detective's first words when General Smith opened the door. "Where are they?"

When he heard they had driven out to the lonely plantation, a look of intense worry came into Mr. Hardy's eyes.

"Their lives are in danger!" he said. The detective quickly introduced Radley, then added, "Come on. We've got to get out there!"

The four ran to the taxi and climbed in. When they pulled away, the general and Chet brought the detectives up to date on the Bush case. At the end, Chet said:

"I have a good clue to Dr. Bush, Mr. Hardy."

"What is it?"

"A picture I took from a plane." The boy showed the photograph of a tall man running. "That's Professor Randolph," he explained. "I'm sure he's Dr. Bush in disguise! Remember the half-picture of him with a black bag I snapped in Bayport?"

"Good work, Chet! I think you're right. Bush and Randolph—his right name's Skagway—*are* one and the same. He's not a professor or a medical doctor, and that black bag contains safecracking tools! He's a bank robber—and deadly." Mr. Hardy leaned toward the taxi driver. "Take her to the limit. Speed may mean the difference between life and death!"

The group sat tensely as the taxi roared toward the plantation.

"There's the car!" Chet announced when they reached the bridge.

As the taxi halted, Mr. Hardy asked the driver to wait. The four passengers dashed toward Rocky Run, along whose banks Frank and Joe had been searching.

Once within cover of the thick overhanging trees, Mr. Hardy called for silence. They pressed forward with barely a sound. The detective and

Radley, accustomed to the job at hand, noiselessly forged ahead of Chet and the general.

Suddenly Mr. Hardy raised his hand. Sam stopped. Voices sounded near them, barely audible above the gurgling of the stream. Through the foliage they could vaguely see the three men who were talking. The trio seemed to be leaning over a hole in the ground.

"I heard the kid say the gold ain't down there!" one of them whined.

A tall man angrily kicked a stone. "That settles it." Then he cried out into the yawning earth, "You've had your last chance, Hardys. We warned your father. Smiley, light the fuse!"

Mr. Hardy and Radley leaped toward the trio. Simultaneously a sharp explosion shook the earth. Rocks and debris shot into the air.

The opening into the tunnel was sealed up!

Chet and the general also came running. Ahead of them stood Randolph-Bush, Junior, and Smiley!

The three men whirled when they heard their pursuers. Junior thrust his gun hand into his pocket. It got no farther. The crashing right fist of Fenton Hardy smashed into Junior's jaw. He sprawled full length.

Randolph took to his heels as Radley made a flying tackle. At the same time Smiley quickly leaned over and snatched a crowbar from the open black bag. He swung at Mr. Hardy. The detective blocked the blow with his left hand. His right slammed against the criminal's midriff. Smiley folded and sank to the ground.

"Get Randolph!" Chet shouted as he saw the ringleader squirm from Radley's shoestring tackle and break away.

He and General Smith were hard after the professor when Mr. Hardy called them back. "We need you here. Quick! Tie these two up, Chet! We have to dig, men, and dig fast!"

Using their hands, pieces of flat stone, and Joe's spade which they had found nearby, they went furiously at the job of freeing Frank and Joe. Fenton Hardy finally crashed through the barrier.

"Frank! Joe!" A moment of silence followed.

Radley's light flashed on the boys. They were lying face down. Neither moved.

Mr. Hardy bent close over his sons. "Thank heaven they're breathing!"

He and Sam Radley carried the boys up the steps. Chet paled. "They're—they're not—"

"No," Mr. Hardy said. "Just knocked out."

He and Radley applied artificial respiration.

Joe opened his eyes first. Then Frank stirred. In a few minutes both boys were on their feet, shaking their heads dazedly. They tried to smile as they related their experience.

"I thought we were dead ducks," Joe said. He shot a glance at the two prisoners who also had regained consciousness. Chet had them well bound and had removed a pistol from Junior's pocket.

"Who's he, Dad?" Frank asked.

"Harold Maskey—called Junior because he looks so young. He's a bad actor."

While Chet was telling the brothers how his picture had identified Randolph as Dr. Bush, that the criminal had been there but had escaped, and that the gang were wanted West Coast bank robbers, Mr. Hardy started back toward the taxi.

"I'm going to advise the State Police to comb this whole area for Bush," he declared.

Suddenly Frank called out, "I'll bet his loot is hidden in the cellar of the Rocky Run Museum. Bush will probably head right there!"

Using the taxi radio, Mr. Hardy was able to get a message through to the police. An officer promised to send men to the museum and a patrol car to pick up the prisoners at Rocky Run. After thanking and paying the taxi driver, the detective returned to the boys.

The captors remained silent. It was not long before three troopers crashed through the woodland to the tunnel. One said news had just come over his car radio that the notorious leader of the bank robbers, posing as Dr. Bush and Professor Randolph, had been found in the cellar of the museum. Secreted in the walls was the West Coast loot. Hank also had confessed. Hearing this, Smiley groaned.

"The jig's up," he said. "If we tell 'em everything, they may go easier on us, Junior."

The two related their part in the plot to get the Smith gold and keep the Hardys out of the case. Their boss, they said, was married to a woman who used to live in the Centerville area and had told him the story of the lost gold. She had not known about her husband's criminal activities until recently, thinking he was off on business trips.

When she had overheard his plans to help himself to the plantation treasure and even go to Bayport to prevent General Smith and the Hardys from coming to Centerville, she had tried to stop him.

"But before she could get the fuzz, he ran off," Smiley smirked.

"So it was Bush's wife who made the phone calls to us," Frank said.

Smiley nodded.

Randolph had helped himself to the secluded museum and threatened the old Negro caretaker and his family. Whenever the robber and his gang wanted to be alone they had locked the old man in a back room.

"How did you find the clue to Pleasanton's Bridge?" Joe asked. "You never saw the message in the bandoleer."

Smiley told them that Randolph, instead of going to town to find out about the deed, had returned to the museum through the cellar and climbed up beneath the old fireplace. There he had eavesdropped, and had heard them mention the bridge.

"Mr. Hardy, I really ain't got no hate against your boys," Smiley concluded. "I got to admit they're smarter'n me."

Such was not the case with Junior. As Sam Radley and the troopers led the two men away, hatred for the Hardys flashed in the youthful-looking criminal's eyes.

When the police car had roared off, Frank said excitedly, "I think we're going to solve the most important mystery—the mystery of the lost tunnel! Follow me!"

By this time the sulphurous air in the cavern had begun to clear. Frank scrambled down the steps, climbing over the debris scattered by the explosion. Joe, Chet, General Smith, and Mr. Hardy followed.

"I still don't get it," Joe said, looking inquiringly at his brother. "There's nothing resembling gold anywhere in here."

Frank led them over to the pile of cannon balls, then stopped. "Remember the message, 'Find coin in iron'? Hold the flashlight, Joe."

Frank opened his knife and scratched the corroding surface of one of the balls. An outer layer began to fall away. Suddenly a glint of gold appeared. Feverishly he scraped off more iron until there was no doubt.

"The treasure!" cried General Smith.

The others gasped in amazement.

Mr. Hardy scraped another ball until the gold winked through. Joe attacked another, Chet a third.

"Great-grandfather's name is vindicated!" the general exclaimed, after examining several more cannon balls to be sure. "The bank will get back its money. And Beauregard's heirs will be able to restore the plantation and can come back to live here!"

Putting his hands on the Hardy boys' shoulders, he turned to their father. "Fenton, you're the luckiest man in the world to have such sons!"

The detective smiled broadly. "You won't find me contradicting you!" He turned to Chet. "Mr. Morton's got a son—and a photographer—to be proud of, too."

Chet beamed as the general slapped him affectionately on the back.

It was not as a photographer, however, that Chet was soon to figure in the Hardys' next adventure, *The Wailing Siren Mystery*.

"Hey! How'd they get the gold inside the cannon balls?" Chet asked.

"They probably melted the gold bars in the blacksmith shop," General Smith answered. "The melting point of gold is very low, you know. Then they either made balls of it and covered them with the iron shells, or else cast hollow cannon balls first and poured in the gold."

"And then plugged the holes," Joe added.

Each of the Hardys and their friends lifted one of the gold cannon balls. As they carried load after load from the lost tunnel, the group chattered gaily.

"I feel so good, I think we ought to have a celebration," Chet asserted.

"With atom crackers?" Frank grinned.

"Or one of Claude's dinners," Joe suggested, his eyes twinkling.

"Oh boy!" Chet exclaimed. "I can hardly wait!"

ORDER FORM

HARDY BOYS MYSTERY SERIES
by Franklin W. Dixon

57 TITLES AT YOUR BOOKSELLER OR COMPLETE AND MAIL THIS HANDY COUPON TO:

GROSSET & DUNLAP, INC.
P.O. Box 941, Madison Square Post Office, New York, N.Y. 10010
Please send me the Hardy Boys Mystery and Adventure Book(s) checked below @ $2.95 each, plus 25¢ *per book* postage and handling. My check or money order for $_____ is enclosed.

1. Tower Treasure — 8901-7	28. The Sign of the Crooked Arrow — 8928-9
2. House on the Cliff — 8902-5	29. The Secret of the Lost Tunnel — 8929-7
3. Secret of the Old Mill — 8903-3	30. Wailing Siren Mystery — 8930-0
4. Missing Chums — 8904-1	31. Secret of Wildcat Swamp — 8931-9
5. Hunting for Hidden Gold — 8905-X	32. Crisscross Shadow — 8932-7
6. Shore Road Mystery — 8906-8	33. The Yellow Feather Mystery — 8933-5
7. Secret of the Caves — 8907-8	34. The Hooded Hawk Mystery — 8934-3
8. Mystery of Cabin Island — 8908-4	35. The Clue in the Embers — 8935-1
9. Great Airport Mystery — 8909-2	36. The Secrets of Pirates Hill — 8936-X
10. What Happened At Midnight — 8910-6	37. Ghost at Skeleton Rock — 8937-8
11. While the Clock Ticked — 8911-4	38. Mystery at Devil's Paw — 8938-6
12. Footprints Under the Window — 8912-2	39. Mystery of the Chinese Junk — 8939-4
13. Mark on the Door — 8913-0	40. Mystery of the Desert Giant — 8940-8
14. Hidden Harbor Mystery — 8914-9	41. Clue of the Screeching Owl — 8941-6
15. Sinister Sign Post — 8915-7	42. Viking Symbol Mystery — 8942-4
16. A Figure in Hiding — 8916-6	43. Mystery of the Aztec Warrior — 8943-2
17. Secret Warning — 8917-3	44. Haunted Fort — 8944-0
18. Twisted Claw — 8918-1	45. Mystery of the Spiral Bridge — 8945-9
19. Disappearing Floor — 8919-X	46. Secret Agent on Flight 101 — 8946-7
20. Mystery of the Flying Express — 8920-3	47. Mystery of the Whale Tattoo — 8947-5
21. The Clue of the Broken Blade — 8921-1	48. The Arctic Patrol Mystery — 8948-3
22. The Flickering Torch Mystery — 8922-X	49. The Bombay Boomerang — 8949-1
23. Melted Coins — 8923-3	50. Danger on Vampire Trail — 8950-5
24. Short-Wave Mystery — 8924-6	51. The Masked Monkey — 8951-3
25. Secret Panel — 8925-4	52. The Shattered Helmet — 8952-3
26. The Phantom Freighter — 8926-2	53. The Clue of the Hissing Serpent — 8953-X
27. Secret of Skull Mountain — 8927-0	54. The Mysterious Caravan — 8954-8
	55. The Witchmaster's Key — 8955-6
	56. The Jungle Pyramid — 8956-4
	57. The Firebird Rocket — 8957-2

SHIP TO:

NAME _____
(please print)

ADDRESS _____

CITY _____ STATE _____ ZIP _____

Printed in U.S.A.   **Please do not send cash.**